Brenna
Lyons

Lovers'
Kiss

FIREBORN
PUBLISHING

Fireborn Publishing Copyright Statement

This book is written in US English.

PUBLISHER

FIREBORN
PUBLISHING

PO Box 5216
Haverhill, MA 01835

A Safe Heart

Prologue to The Color of Love

Grace Mallory stared at the half-empty glass of white wine...her second thus far, running her finger along the upper edge of the crystal.

"Something wrong, Grace?" Josh asked.

Besides the fact that I'd rather be drinking a beer? Of course, Joshua Winters would probably be shocked, if she ordered barley and hops with a seventy-dollar meal. For him, it was the finest vintages, yet another difference between Josh and Michael.

She shook that thought away, masking it as a negative response, pasted on a smile and raised her glass to her dinner companion. *Forget the past. Josh is the present. There's no reason to compare them. Michael is gone.*

"It's Justice again, isn't it?" he asked, setting his glass down and picking up his fork. His grip was light, nearly pretty in its elegance.

Grace wanted to deny it, but there was little point. Josh had waited three months to approach her about furthering the relationship between them. Though he didn't want to be a rebound, he knew she was hurting and would for a little longer.

Unlike Michael, Josh had a heart and could appreciate such things. Josh wasn't clumsy. He wasn't without perception and empathy.

"It still stings. I guess it will, for a while," she offered.

"You don't just turn off your feelings," he agreed, twisting his fork in the perfect primavera.

The perfect primavera. The perfect man. So, why doesn't it feel like it sometimes? Why do I still think of Michael? It was insane. No rational person would be thinking about Michael Justice, after what he did. At least she could honestly say she didn't want him.

"If you don't mind me asking..." Josh glanced up at her, assessing her mood.

"No. Go on."

"How did you ever fall in with Justice? I would never have pegged the two of you as compatible."

"I suppose we weren't," Grace conceded. Which made her feelings all the more incomprehensible.

"How did it happen?" He went back to his meal, giving Grace space to choose to answer...or not.

Space... Did Michael ever give me space?

~

"Really? This is no joke?" Michael asked.

Grace nodded. "I told you that Adam Silver is a fan."

Convincing the art critic to detour to cover Michael's show hadn't been difficult. Not that Grace was going to tell Michael how easy it had been. If he thought she'd had to do some major wheeling and dealing to pull this off, let him think it.

"Grace...I...you really—"

She smiled at his stumbling. For once, she'd left Michael Justice speechless. Grace had never met a more self-assured man. He was gorgeous, buff, talented, intelligent, and good-natured. What was there not to be self-assured about?

His hands cupped her head, and his mouth closed on hers. Grace's surprise was drowned out by an uncompromising arousal.

She'd wanted Michael Justice since the first time he'd set foot in Le Artiste; this response was too good to be true. Grace pressed her hands flat to his chest and opened her lips wider, moaning as he deepened the kiss.

The faux ivory pins holding her hair up eased out then clattered onto the edge of her desk. Her hair loosened then unfurled, the weight sliding along her shoulders and back. Michael buried his hands in its length, fisting then releasing it, exhaling hard against her cheek.

Grace slipped her arms up, circling his neck and bringing herself flush to his body...and to the erection straining his jeans. Anne had already left for the day, and she'd never been more glad of the fact.

Any speculations about his intentions were laid to rest. The man had the most unquestionably carnal nature she'd ever encountered, and Grace loved it. In a heartbeat, she knew Michael wouldn't be stopping, and she didn't want him to.

As if stating his agreement, he yanked up at her skirt, uncovering her to her hips. The fingertips of his left hand traced the tops of her thigh-high stockings then retreated.

His lips left hers, and their eyes met. The question was asked and answered that simply, intent and agreement.

With a nod of his head, Michael lifted Grace to her desktop and leaned over her, pushing papers and pens aside as she sank beneath him. His jeans were open and pushed away before she had her bearings again. Her panties were at her knees a heartbeat later.

He lodged himself inside her with a moan and a shiver. Grace levered her legs up, kicking away her heels and panties, intent on wrapping them around him. Michael had other ideas; he grasped her beneath the knees and forced her legs up and apart.

Before she could question him, he was pistoning in and out of her. Not that Grace intended to complain about it. Not while she was skyrocketing to climax.

Her brain ceased to function, awash in waves of sensual stimuli. Gasping cries that might have contained fractured pleas for more gave way to a full-throated scream of release that scorched at her lungs and throat.

Michael grumbled and grunted out something that made no sense to her. He froze inside her then raised Grace until she was chest to chest with him again, teetering on the edge of her desk, the plane of his hips and the length of his cock holding her in place.

Grace thumbed several buttons on his denim shirt open and parted it to reveal his chest. He seemed to hold his breath, while she lowered her face, pressing her lips to his skin. The taste of his salt-heavy sweat and musk had barely registered on her savoring tongue when he was moving again.

She reached her toes out, grasping the arms of her desk chair and reeling it in, thanking some unnamed deity that she'd opted for a chair that didn't roll at the heavy executive desk and one that did at her smaller work station.

The fact that it didn't roll meant she could plant her feet on it and move against Michael, setting a furious pace to off-the-charts pleasure. Michael's climax was as frantic as the rest, hot jets of come buffeting her while he continued to thrust into her.

Then, they were still in each other's arms, breathing harshly, rumpled, sweat-soaked and, at least for Grace, still not sated. Michael's breath teased at her swollen lips, his words easing inside, following the paths his tongue once had.

"Dear God, I've been dreaming about that for weeks."

She nodded. Grace had been dreaming of it too, but she'd never dared hope Michael would... *Rock my world?* Oh, but he had done that.

And, she wanted it again. Grace went back to unbuttoning his shirt, trailing her lips over ridges of muscles drawn tight in arousal.

Michael went to work on her blouse, playing at her breasts through her bra, still deliciously hard inside her. "Satin," he noted. "Nice."

Grace pushed his sleeves down his arms, and he released her with a grumbled complaint, tearing the clothing off and returning to his exploration. In a few dizzying moments, she was stripped to the waist.

"Better," he breathed. His hands cupped her breasts, his thumbs brushing over her nipples, sending ripples of delight through her belly.

"Yes. It is." Her voice hardly seemed her own, low, husky, pure invitation. She'd never played the wanton before. There was something liberating in just letting passion unfold, expand...explode.

His cock jerked, and she closed her eyes, arching against him.

Let it happen. Whatever he's planning, just go with it. Worry about where it takes you later.

Michael slid from her body, and she opened her eyes, shaking her head and moaning in protest. Her counsel of following where Michael led didn't extend to following him to an early end, apparently.

Grace wrapped her legs around him, and he smiled widely, moving closer as she tightened her thigh muscles and drew him in. There was something knowing in that smile, something wicked and taunting that made her blood heat again.

He unwrapped her legs and spread them wide, licking his lips as he surveyed the length of her body. His cock brushed the sensitized slit still aching for him.

"Before this goes in again, we're both going to be naked," he informed her.

Grace swallowed hard, meeting his dark blue eyes. She flicked a glance at his erection, and it bucked in response.

Let it happen. For once, don't think. "Then we better get moving on that."

His voice was so low, she almost missed his response.

"I don't know what I did right, but I swear to God, I'll do it again."

A smiled pulled up at her lips. "I certainly hope so," she purred.

Grace unhooked then unzipped her skirt, swiveling her hips as she pushed it away to let it fall to the floor. Michael released her legs and watched it drop.

His hands returned, working their way beneath her stockings and peeling them off, kneading her legs as they eased away. They landed somewhere behind him, but neither of them paid them any attention.

Green eyes were locked with blue, something nameless growing between them.

~

"Grace?" Josh inquired, a note of concern in his voice. The backs of his fingertips trailed along the line of her jaw.

She started then smiled. "It just happened, Josh. Sometimes, life hits you, when you don't expect it."

His smile wasn't brittle and hard. It was soft, nurturing. He tucked an escaping lock of hair back into her bun. "We don't have to discuss it, if you don't want to."

That brought out a more natural smile in her. "I'd appreciate that."

"You know I'd never force you to talk about something you don't want to," he reminded her, a touch of hurt in his tone.

"Of course." They'd been friends before they were lovers. They'd been friends before Michael...and after Michael and were now. They likely always would be.

Josh leaned toward her, feathering his lips over hers, parting them carefully. The kiss was slow and deep, a promise of the night to come. When he pulled back, his eyes glittered in renewal of that same promise.

He went back to his meal, and Grace noted that he was nearly done, when she'd barely picked at her own.

"I take it you aren't hungry tonight, Grace?" he asked, probably believing it a safe subject.

Her stomach clenched uncomfortably. "Unfortunately, no."

"Dessert to go?" he offered.

"If you'd like some. I'll pass, thanks."

Josh cocked his head, examining her for a moment, as if she presented a logic problem to him. "Shall we retire to my place?"

A little thrill went through her at the thought of Josh's undivided attention to her. Where sex was concerned, 'undivided' was one word that surely applied to him.

"That's the best idea I've heard all day," she admitted.

"I'm glad."

He waved for the check and signed to have it added to his club tab. In minutes, he was whisking her away to bliss.

Bliss wouldn't come in moments, of course. Josh was the type to wait until they were comfortably ensconced in a bed, clothing hung or folded nearby, condom in place...safe and comfortable, in every way.

Quickies weren't in his repertoire, either. When Josh committed to sex, he planned to take his time and do it right, which meant his full focus and determination on the goal of them both enjoying the night fully.

As they waited for the car, Josh indulged in another preparatory kiss. It did its job well, rendering her slick and aching for more, wiping the bittersweet memories of fast fucks and careless words from her mind.

She slid into the car next to him, letting her eyes wander his impeccably-kept appearance. Josh was her friend and her lover. Best of all, Josh was safe.

If there was one thing Michael Justice taught her, it was that nothing was more important than a safe heart. If she didn't wake from dreams of him, all the better. It meant she wasn't disturbed.

The Color of Love

Chapter One

November 16

"Package, Miss," the delivery man intoned.

Grace took the clipboard without looking up and signed the virtual screen. The plastic board was lifted away and the small box deposited on the counter in front of her, silently and efficiently, as most deliveries were made at the art gallery.

She didn't look at it immediately. It was probably some trinket to be placed in the gem art displays, which meant less room in the rapidly-filling safe. So intent was she on her paperwork that Grace nearly walked away from it entirely.

"Not smart," she muttered, turning back. She hadn't made a name for herself with artists by losing their work, and she wasn't about to start now. She stuffed the box in her deep jacket pocket and ambled toward her office.

Anne was working at the cleaning stand, a surprisingly popular exhibit. No one who'd ever restored art could have imagined how interested buyers would be in seeing it accomplished, and sales of older pieces had risen almost twenty percent since she'd instituted it.

Grace set the package on the work table next to Anne's swabs. "Do me a favor and log this in. And if it needs any work—"

She laughed. "Yeah, I know. The Gemstone Tea is only three weeks away. Everything will be ready, Grace. You know it will."

"That's why I trust you to do this." She turned away, checking her watch. There was still time to finalize the menu with the caterer, before he closed for the evening. Everything would be perfect. It was the only way she ran a show.

The Gemstone Tea will be well-attended. The sales might carry us for a full six months.

"Grace?" Anne called out.

She sighed, hoping there was no major damage to the shipment. "Yes?"

"I don't think this box is for the exhibit."

That brought her out of her circling thoughts and concerns. "Then what is it?"

"I don't know, but it's not addressed to *Le Artiste.* It's addressed to you. Are you sure you want me to open this?"

Grace looked back in surprise. "Me?" Why would anyone send her a package at the gallery? Portfolio folders or letters of introduction were often addressed to her as the gallery owner, but not packages.

"Grace Elizabeth Mallory."

She smiled at the joke. "They did not use my full name." No one used her full name, not even her mother.

"Actually, whoever sent this did."

"How strange." She strode back to the table and plucked the box from it.

It was tiny, smaller around than her palm. Sure enough, the box was addressed, in miniscule printed lettering, to her. There was no return address, not that there was room for one. Grace ripped the brown paper off, opened the lid and pulled out a bit of blank newsprint paper, uncovering a jeweler's ring box.

"Oh my," she managed, setting the box down again.

Anne's eyes lit up with glee. "Do you think this is Mr. Winters' way of proposing to you?"

Grace's heart pounded. "Joshua? No. I don't think so. I mean, he wouldn't..." *Would he? No. Not Josh.* "Not this way, I'm sure." It was way too flighty and...and inappropriate. One thing Josh was known for was his impeccable appearances. If he ever decided to propose, it would be in the most expensive restaurant in Boston, on one knee, with a velvet pillow beneath it.

"Maybe a friendship ring then," she suggested. "Open it. You have to look, Grace."

She nodded, pulling the ring box free and flipping the lid open. A folded sheet of paper flipped down over the ring, and she caught it between her index and middle fingers, staring at the ring beneath. It was certainly no engagement ring.

Grace furrowed her brow, stunned at her relief at that. She pushed away the unwelcome realization and pulled the ring out of the box.

It was a white gold band etched with Celtic knotwork. The stone was a teardrop shape, the top smooth and gleaming, crystal clear and reflecting the white gold backing.

"Lovely," she murmured.

Despite her current show, gemstones weren't Grace's usual line, and she couldn't begin to imagine what type of stone it was. If it was quartz crystal, it was higher quality than most she'd seen...and more stunning. There was no way that it was diamond. The stone had to be at least two carats, and even Josh wouldn't spend that for anything but an engagement ring.

Grace slid the ring on her right ring finger, admiring it. She gasped, dropping the paper in surprise as the stone started to change color.

"What is it?" Anne asked.

"It's... It's a mood ring. My God! It's been years since I've seen one."

Anne crowded next to her, her freckled nose scrunched up. Grace half expected her to grab the magnifying glasses from the tabletop.

"It's odd, though," her assistant noted.

"What is?" The stone settled on a peaceful peach color.

"Most mood rings are just a clear stone with a film of heat-sensitive metal beneath. Looking down on it, it seems to change color, but looking at it from the side, it's still a clear stone."

It turned light gray. Grace stared at it, smiling as it turned bright sky blue. "And?"

"Look at it from the side, Grace."

She lifted her hand and turned it slowly, watching the entire stone shift from sky blue to Hunter green. "The whole stone changes," she noted. "The whole stone is sensitive?" What kind of stone did that? None that she knew of.

* * * *

"Ohhh. How wonderful," Anne squealed.

Grace rolled her eyes. "I *do* have to get some work

done," she suggested for the third time. As it was, she'd missed the caterer and had to add it to her overloaded schedule for the following day.

Anne ran a finger down the paper that had been folded in the ring box. It turned out that it wasn't a note from the sender, which was still a mystery, but rather an ornate, hand-calligraphed list of the colors the stone would take on and their meanings. "But, it's turning orange, which means... No. Yellow. Oh..."

"What?" Grace snapped.

"I'm annoying you, aren't I?"

"What was your first clue?"

"Uh... The ring turning yellow. It's never wrong, you know."

"Anne," she pleaded.

"Well, it isn't. Look at the colors you've seen so far. Peach..." She bit her lip, panning her eyes downward. "Well, that means either friendship or fond remembrance. Weren't you saying how long it had been since you'd seen a mood ring?"

"Yes, but—"

Anne motioned for patience. "Gray... That's confusion, and sky blue is happiness. Hunter green is surprise."

"You've been keeping track of every change?" she asked incredulously.

"Watch it. You'll see." Anne handed the instruction sheet over and headed out of the office.

Grace stared at the paper uneasily, her eyes straying to the ring again. "Butter yellow." She scanned down the list of colors and meanings. "Nervous. Delightful." Anne was right. The ring was never wrong.

* * * *

Grace pulled into the parking garage under her apartment building, sighing as she turned off the car. Despite her best intentions, she'd gotten very little work done since the ring crossed her path.

It was a mad obsession of sorts. Over and over again, she'd taken the ring off, determined that she wouldn't sacrifice hours of time to some trinket. It never lasted long. Invariably, she'd put the ring on again, trying to prove it was wrong. It never was.

Well, dinner wasn't going to cook itself. She dragged herself out of the car and locked the door with the key fob remote. The walk to the elevator then down the hall to her apartment seemed longer than usual.

Grace tried to convince herself that she was simply tired, but she wasn't. There was no question about that. She was distracted, nervous, any number of things the damned ring would tell her. The worst part was, she knew she'd look at it.

Inside her apartment, Grace kicked off her shoes and stripped off her winter coat, leaving both in the front hall. Why not? Josh was out of town on business. He wouldn't be stopping by to scold her about her almost non-existent housekeeping skills.

She let down her hair and shook the long, brown ringlets around her face. It felt great to shed the last vestiges of the office and simply enjoy the silence around her.

Her dinner was already prepared and in the fridge as usual. All she had to do was pop it in the oven and prepare tomorrow night's dinner while it cooked. Overall, Grace figured that the seemingly-backward system saved her an average of an hour or so per night, and with her commitments, time was priceless.

The timer set and the oven heating, the stew along with it, she pulled the chicken she'd defrosted out of the fridge, placed a package of pork chops from the freezer in its place, and set about making the cheese sauce it would bake in.

Grace stilled, the blinking light on the answering machine catching her attention. Who would be calling her now?

Josh wouldn't call until nine; he always assumed she'd work late and didn't want to waste time and money on her answering machine. That was Josh, all right...practical to a fault.

She scowled at the realization that he had no apparent faults, and dealing with a seemingly perfect person was somewhere between daunting and annoying some days.

So, it isn't Josh. Who else did that leave?

Her mother only called on Sundays, so it wasn't Mom.

Her sister wasn't the calling type; Valerie only communicated via e-mail and instant messaging, unless forced at gunpoint to do otherwise.

Anne and Elizabeth had both left the gallery before she did, so it wasn't a problem there. In case of a break-in, the security company would have paged her.

Grace sighed. With no doctors' appointments that would need confirmed, that left only a telemarketer or similar annoyance. Better to get it over with and enjoy the rest of the evening. She hit the play button and went back to slicing the block of cheddar.

"Message one. Tuesday. Six PM."

"Grace? Are you there?"

The knife slipped and sliced into her finger. *Oh, no. Life is simply not this unfair.*

"It's Michael Justice, Grace."

As if I could ever forget your voice?

He tapped the mouthpiece on the phone, and she could picture him doing it. Looking around the room...wherever he was, his rich brown hair tussled, his fingernail clicking against the edge of the phone. It was an old nervous habit of his.

Is he nervous?

Grace shoved that thought out of her mind violently. Whether or not he was nervous was none of her concern! Michael was the one who'd chosen to end their relationship. It was over, and his feelings were no longer her problem.

"I hope you're not avoiding me."

His voice was dark and sensual, an unspoken promise to come up with a suitable sexual torture for her peeking from behind the surface of the discussion. How many times had he...

Stop that! You promised yourself there was no coming back. You promised yourself that you wouldn't be waiting for Michael like a puppy at the door.

And, she wasn't waiting for him. There was Josh, now.

His finger tapped again, several quick jerking movements. "I have to see you, Grace. I have a lot to tell you."

The message ended with a beep, and she sucked in air raggedly, abruptly aware that she wasn't breathing. She turned to the sink, pouring her attention into cleaning and bandaging the cut then mopping up the blood on the countertop with a sponge.

His words circled in her mind, echoing until all she could think about was Michael and the idea of seeing him again. There would be no avoiding that. Michael always got what he wanted.

"Except me back," she vowed.

Grace glanced at the ring, groaning aloud. She didn't have to ask what pink meant. If her rock-hard nipples, goose bumps and damp panties were any indication, pink meant arousal.

Chapter Two

November 17

Grace stirred her tea absently, visions of Michael dancing in her head.

Typically, being secluded in her office, away from the desk and her usual patrons, focused her into the almost endless work of running the gallery, but not today. Not since the ring came into her life.

She grimaced. Not since Michael called and said he wanted to see her. *No! He said he had to see me.*

Grace ran her fingertips over her desk. It had been the first place they'd made love, a wild, passionate encounter that marked the start of the fourteen most carefree months of her life.

She growled, cursing herself for her weakness. Michael had hurt her when he'd left, and Grace had promised herself she wouldn't fall for his charm again.

The ring caught her eye, pearly pink announcing her arousal again. "Damn it." Couldn't the stupid thing lie to agree with her, just once?

Grace pulled it off her finger and tossed it on the desk. The stone went clear with amazing speed, as it always did when it left her body. She tried to ignore it, tried to concentrate on the RSVPs for the Gemstone Tea, but it kept drawing her eyes back to it, like a magnet with filings.

She sighed. It was a mood ring. There was no mystery about it. Like Anne said, it was simply sensitive to temperature changes.

A smile broke free. If she proved it was nothing more than a glorified thermometer, she could stop acting like the damned thing was magic. Her tea would be perfect. It was warm and not steaming. Yes...it would do just fine.

The stone turned orange as soon as her fingers closed around the band, and her mind supplied the translation, curiosity. Grace dropped the ring in the clear crystal cup—and her smile disappeared. The stone went clear as soon as it left her hand. Worse, it stayed clear.

Some rational corner of her mind argued that it might be a light peach or butter that she couldn't see because of the tea. She fished it out with the spoon, staring at the undeniably clear stone in confusion.

"It's not based on heat," she mumbled. What else could it be sensitive to? *Possibly electrical current.* Grace considered the cord for the old touchier lamp she intended to replace seriously for a moment.

No! That is truly insane! You are not going to play electrician and strip wires just to test the stupid ring.

She startled at a knock on the door, dropping the ring back in the tea then spooning it back up, dropping it twice in the process. She dried it on her kerchief, looked at the telltale stain on the linen then stuffed it in her jacket pocket, shoving the ring back on her finger. The stone turned Navy blue, and her cheeks heated at the completely unnecessary announcement that she was embarrassed to be nearly caught trying to prove this silly piece of junk was a fake.

"Oh, shut up," she grumbled at it, wincing that she was talking to an inanimate object.

"Grace?" Anne called out.

"Yes?" Grace rubbed at the tension in her forehead. She'd spoken in too falsely cheery a voice. Anne wouldn't buy that for a second.

"There's *someone* here to see you."

"I really am too busy today." *And anyone I want to see will have made an appointment. Take that, Michael.*

"Excuse me. You can't just barge in there," Anne protested.

Grace looked up, half in exasperation and half in dismay, as the door swung in and Michael strode through, a mocking smile on his face. His dark eyes nearly gleamed in unspoken challenge.

Michael gets whatever he wants, she reminded herself. *Except me!*

She waved Anne away, before the younger woman could offer to call security for her, turning her attention back to him as the door closed. "You really should learn to make an appointment, Mr. Justice," she offered coolly.

He ignored the barb, striding across the room and sitting in one of the client chairs, dragging his fingertips along the edge of the desk suggestively. He was abruptly serious. She forced her breathing to even as his eyes darkened, certain that he was remembering countless ways that they'd enjoyed the desk...and the chairs.

Why had she never changed them out for new furniture? She had the money to redecorate and had considered it several times. To prove that he had no power over her? Perhaps to prove that it meant nothing to her?

It doesn't! "You don't have an appointment," she reminded him, "and I'm very busy."

"Would you have given me one?" he countered, his mouth curving up into a wicked smile.

No! "Of course. Your art is very popular with many of my patrons."

His eyes flicked down her body then up again as if taking stock of any changes since he'd been gone, not that there were many. "You are a horrible liar. You always were."

Grace schooled her expression, though she felt her cheeks heat. "Your right to claim familiarity with my emotions was forfeited last year."

His smile disappeared. "You're right. It was, but—"

"Are you here for some reason besides a lame come-on, which I assure you, I will turn down?"

Michael stared at her in seeming shock that fueled her dislike of him. How long had it been since he had been on the receiving end of a dump? Maybe the experience would do him good.

"Yes. Of course, I am. I *am* an artist, and you were a gallery owner, last time I checked."

Her breathing hitched. *What? You expected him to say he'd come to see you? Just you? That he can't live without you? That giving you up was the worst mistake he's ever made?* Well, it would have been a good start!

"Grace—"

"Just a moment." She wrenched her side drawer open, rifling through the files until she came up with a blank show packet. She pushed it across the desk, keeping her hands far from his and pulling them back the moment he had a hold on the forms.

The last thing she wanted was him trying to comfort her in some awkward, clumsy Michael way. The man chose the worst words he could in almost every situation. *Like the night he left.*

No. That had been planned.

"Gr—"

"The forms haven't changed much in the last year. You know how to fill them out." *He should after two shows here.* "Just drop them off to Anne when you bring them back." *My clients like Michael's work, and a Michael Justice show combined with the Gemstone Tea will carry the gallery another nine months, without breaking a sweat.* That meant she could afford the alarm upgrades she wanted.

"Don't you want to see the paintings before you agree to this?"

Grace ignored him. "Would January the thirteenth be agreeable to you? Or do you need more time to complete your offerings? A Michael Justice show is always easy to populate, so the short notice will be no problem, and everyone is looking for something to do at that time of year." *And the sooner the show is over and he's out of my life, the better for me.*

"No. They're ready. The thirteenth is fine, but..." He sighed.

"But?" she replied, feigning interest in her calendar to hide her hurt.

"You should see the paintings before you agree to this." He sounded confused, perhaps even hesitant.

No. Michael Justice is never hesitant. "December the twentieth at six o'clock," she offered without looking up.

"All right. If you really want to wait that long."

Grace flicked her pen open. "How many paintings will you be showing?"

"If you accept only the main body of works, I can

fill the front gallery. The full showing would also fill the Rounde and the blue room."

She fisted her pen, calculating the number of paintings he'd completed in the past year in disbelief. "I guess you were right," she managed. Ending their relationship was obviously the boost his muse needed. She'd been holding him back.

"Grace... I—I really should explain."

"That won't be necessary, Mr. Justice. I'll see you on December twentieth. You can approve the invitations that night."

"Or before," he grumbled.

"I don't think that's wise."

"You're avoiding me."

She didn't answer. Why should it surprise him that she didn't want to spend time with him after the things he'd said? Especially since he'd been right about her influence. The man wanted his art, and now he had it back. That should be enough for each of them.

Michael rose and strode to the door, opening it. He paused with the knob still encased in his fist, his back fully to her. "I know you're hurt, and that's my fault. Sooner or later, we have to discuss this."

"It's ancient history. There is nothing left to discuss. You said it best. You are an artist. I am a gallery owner. End of subject."

"You never were a good liar." He stepped through the door and disappeared down the hall.

Grace dropped her pen, burying her face in her hands. She would not allow herself to cry. Not over Michael Justice. She'd done more than her share of that, and she didn't intend to start again now.

She lowered her hands to the desktop, forcing a

semblance of calm to her general appearance much as she had in the months after he'd left. A groan built in her throat, escaping as the ring's lavender stone called her a liar.

"Longing," she noted miserably. After the hell he'd put her through and all the rational arguments, she still wanted him. The fact that he was poison to her didn't seem to factor into it, in the least.

* * * *

Michael slammed his studio door behind him, pacing the floor in frustration. He cursed himself a dozen types of fool, creep and general asshole within a two minute period.

Leaving Grace had been a stupid move. He'd been a coward, afraid of how much he needed her, afraid of admitting that their fling had become something more, afraid he'd painted their relationship with impossible colors that would turn dun and gray when they'd had time to set.

It was true that he hadn't been painting much at the time, but he'd lied about Grace hampering his creativity. She inspired him, but she inspired him to paint pieces unlike anything he'd ever painted before.

Gone were the angsty pieces in blues and browns. Suddenly, his canvas sang with reds, coral and gold, vibrant colors, full of life and light...like Grace was. He looked toward his failed attempts at recapturing his old form in disgust. Grace had spoiled him on it, and at the time, that thought had terrified him.

Michael laughed harshly at his own folly. The idea of wiping away Grace's influence by wiping Grace out of his life had been born out of desperation, ill conceived and poorly executed.

The things he'd said to her that winter night had been nothing short of cruel. He couldn't even remember why he'd wanted to hurt her so badly. The only plausible excuse, sad as it was, was that he was hurting, and he didn't like the fact that he was. Or, maybe he was blaming Grace for making him hurt? But, whether he was blaming her for the fact that losing his art as he knew it hurt or losing her hurt, he couldn't begin to untangle.

Of course, there was the truly mad possibility that he thought the hurting would bring back the dark muse. Perhaps he even welcomed the pain in hopes of it...or in hopes of making some amends for hurting Grace.

Hurting hadn't brought back the old style. Loneliness hadn't engendered a single blue painting. Even moving to his parents' place in Hartford for six months, where every corner of his surroundings didn't remind him of Grace, hadn't done the trick; all that had done was annoyed him with his mother's attempts to marry him off while he was under her roof.

He'd tried to force himself to abandon the new style, even tried to copy his older works for practice. His hand had shaken so severely that he could hardly hold the brush.

No, Michael could paint bold reds and gold through bitter tears or in rare moments of peace. He lived the lemon light, dreamed the coral vitality, breathed the crimson energy of his new style. Through it all, Grace was never far from his mind. Everywhere he looked, he encountered proof that he'd made a mistake.

He had to get her back, but her pain ran deep. His only ray of hope in their meeting had been when the ring turned lavender. Despite his actions, she wanted him. As long as that was true, he'd never stop trying to win her back.

Chapter Three

November 19

Michael strolled down River Street, shifting the paperwork in his hand nervously. He had to see Grace to win her back, but how was he going to convince Anne to disturb her, when Grace had no doubt given orders not to admit him again?

He couldn't fake a question about the paperwork. With five years of shows at various galleries and two at *Le Artiste*, there was no clause he could pretend not to understand. In addition, Anne could answer any question he had...or deal with any reasonable request.

Playing the prima donna would backfire in two ways. First, it was still almost two months until his show. Any changes he demanded could be handled by Anne and Elizabeth without involving Grace. The upcoming Gemstone Tea would be her primary concern. It was a showcase of artists, some new to her patrons, and Grace worked best under pressure.

Second... He sighed. Grace loathed prima donnas. Acting the spoiled artist with her would only hurt his chances.

Well, what do you think you did a year ago?

He winced at the sight of Le Artiste, wishing that he'd walked slower. He couldn't stand around outside, considering his course. He'd just have to wing it.

Another man reached the door just before him and released it into Michael's hand without a backward glance. They approached the desk a few steps apart.

Anne looked up, her brow creased in an expression Michael couldn't quite get a handle on.

The other man spoke in cool tones, as Michael came even with him. "Good afternoon, Anne. Would you tell Grace I'm here, please?"

"Of course, Mr. Winters."

Michael bit back a curse. Grace had an appointment. That blew his chance to see her to hell. Now, how was he going to explain another visit to the gallery? *I'm just checking out the competition, honestly. Oh, that sucks!*

Anne pushed the button on the intercom. "Grace, Mr. Winters is here to see you, and—"

"I'll be right out."

Anne's eyes widened. "No, you—" She groaned aloud, grimacing as the office door swung open and Grace strode out, her hips swaying enticingly.

Michael swallowed a laugh painfully. If Grace was intent on ducking him, she'd have to get a lot better at picking up warning clues from her employees.

"Josh! I'm so glad you're back." She glanced at her watch. "Your plane must have been early."

"Believe it or not, one-twenty-eight was absolutely clear sailing."

She reached his side and rose on tiptoe, planting a kiss on the man's tanned cheek. "You came straight here from the airport? How sweet of you."

Michael rolled his eyes, scowling at his rival. Josh Winters hardly looked like a man who'd just come from a plane ride. His sun-streaked blonde hair was perfectly coifed, and his business suit seemed freshly pressed. How could this putz possibly keep up with a passionate woman like Grace?

She settled on her heels again, and her eyes locked on Michael's. The smile faded from her face. "Mr. Justice," she greeted him in a voice that nearly matched Winters' form of address for Anne. "I trust Anne is taking care of you."

"Not yet. I just arrived."

Grace nodded. "Well, then... I have a prior engagement, so I'll leave you in her hands."

Liar! She hadn't even known pretty boy was coming in. In addition to what she'd said to Winters only moments earlier, the catch in her voice and the movements of her eyes announced clearly that she wasn't telling him the truth.

Michael pretended not to notice Anne's hand reaching for the contract. He was too busy playing 'size up the competition' with a pair of ice blue eyes. Not that there was much to it. Winters dismissed his jeans, hiking boots, barn jacket and paint-stained, Mandarin-collar denim shirt nearly as quickly as Michael dismissed him.

"Justice?" Winters mused. "Would you be Michael Justice?"

"I would." *Delightful. Yuppie Jr. is going to make a gallant attempt to defend his lady's honor.*

He sniffed, an arrogant sound of dislike. "Yes. I've heard of you."

Michael raised an eyebrow at that, nearly daring Winters to say something about the shameful way he'd treated Grace.

"Brilliant artiste, of course, but you're not a very personable sort, I hear. The truly successful artistes mingle with their patrons, you know."

It was on the tip of his tongue to retort that he and

Grace tended to christen each of his shows on her desk, and keeping his hands and mouth off of her had never seemed all that important to him at the time, that the "glow" the art columnists talked about when she hosted one of his shows was sexual afterglow.

He didn't say it, of course. Her blush and the Navy blue stone in her ring let him know how embarrassing she already found the conversation. "I'll take that under advisement," he managed in what would pass for a civil tone—to anyone but Grace.

She bit her lip lightly, and the stone morphed to a soft butter yellow. Was she worried that he'd cause a scene? Michael knew better than that. Nothing would cook his chances faster than causing a scene here.

Deliberately, as if staking a claim on her, Winters lowered his face and captured Grace's mouth with his. For an instant, she stiffened. Then she wound her arms around his neck and pressed closer to him. The kiss left no doubt that they were lovers. It wasn't as unrestrained as the kisses she'd shared with Michael, but it was certainly involved. Grace had never been a good liar, even in action.

Michael ground his teeth in frustration. Why had he never considered that she might care for someone else by now? She'd had a year to move on, and she was a desirable woman.

She ran her fingers through Winters' hair, and Michael found his eyes drawn to the ring, half-dreading what it would say about her feelings for the man who held her so close to him that he was probably wrinkling his pristine suit.

Michael relaxed so abruptly that he had to steady himself against the counter, though he thought he covered that well enough as a casual move. He bit back the urge to laugh out loud. The ring was a muddied color somewhere between peach and rose, friendship and affection. It was far too dark to be pink arousal and far too light to be red love. He still had a chance.

Grace broke away, studiously avoiding Michael's eyes. The ring returned to Navy blue, practically shouting that she was more than aware of him watching that kiss.

Winters smiled widely, straightening his still-unrumpled suit and smoothing his hair. "Ready for lunch?" he asked, offering her his arm.

She wound her hand through and headed to the door without a backward glance...or a coat or purse. Michael fought back a fresh wave of jealousy and handed the contracts to Anne.

* * * *

Grace sighed in relief as Josh closed the car door behind her. At least that scene was over with. Michael would have no more reason to come to the gallery for a few more weeks. He certainly wouldn't pursue her, now that Josh had made their relationship clear.

Or had he? She stared at the ring's shifting colors. Watching the ring was nearly addictive. Grace had admitted that to herself days earlier, though she couldn't fathom why it would be. The damned thing kept telling her what she didn't want to hear, after all.

Now, for instance... The stone kept shifting between gray confusion and purple despair. It just wasn't fair! Michael Justice had no right to confuse her or make her miserable. He'd done more than his share of it, and he certainly wasn't due more than that.

She considered canceling his show. She hadn't signed the contract, yet. It was still possible to send him packing, but this wasn't the right time for a move like that. His show would bring in good money, and canceling would give him a wide open field to take pot shots at her and her business. While she'd like to believe that he wouldn't stoop to that, she didn't know what to expect from him. How often did Michael Justice lose?

Josh settled into the driver's seat, and she offered him a strained smile. He seemed to consider her carefully for a moment. "Call Pietro's, will you?"

Grace stared at him. "Pietro's will be packed at this time of day," she reminded him. If there was one thing Josh couldn't abide, it was waiting in line at a noisy, crowded restaurant. 'Reservations' was practically his middle name.

"We won't be eating there. They'll be delivering..." He glanced at her again then turned his eyes forward, starting the engine and swinging out onto the side street that would lead up to River. "To my place."

Her heart skipped a beat at that, visions of Josh shedding his usual tactician control and ravishing her in his living room making her breathing labor and her head spin. Realization that she was projecting encounters with Michael onto Josh and looking forward to them shocked her back to reality.

This was Josh. It wasn't Michael. Josh was safe, dependable, easy to anticipate. Josh didn't do things like stripping away clothes and sending them flying. He didn't lift her onto her desk and...

And, he won't break my heart! That's why he's safe.

She didn't delve into why he wouldn't break her heart. Josh just wouldn't do it, and that was enough.

"Grace?" he reminded her.

She pulled the cell phone from her jacket pocket, fumbling a bit as she opened it and started pecking in the number from memory. "Your usual?" she asked.

"Of course."

She nodded, placing the order with only half of her mind on the task. *His usual.* It was another reminder of why she enjoyed being with Josh. Strange that she couldn't seem to find as much comfort in it as she usually did.

They traveled the distance to his condo in silence, up the elevator and inside. Josh closed the door and took her suit jacket, hanging it neatly in the closet then his own.

He marched into the kitchen, back straight, regimental as always, and returned with two glasses— filtered water for himself and Classic Coke for her. Though he couldn't stand soda personally, he always kept a six pack of cans on hand for her visits.

Grace wasn't in the mood for Coke; her stomach was churning well enough without the added caffeine, but she took it and sank onto one end of the couch, sipping it for show.

Josh joined her, trailing his gaze from her feet to face slowly. "You still want him," he noted.

She choked on a mouthful of the Coke in surprise, accepting a napkin from him, blotting her lips and blouse carefully to avoid meeting his eyes. Grace searched frantically for the words to deny it.

"You do want him. Don't you?"

Her cheeks heated. "I'm not stupid, Josh. Michael

is no good. Not for me, anyway. I know that. I have no intention of—"

"Then why do you want him?"

Grace didn't answer him. Why did Josh have to be so damned rational about the whole thing? Why couldn't he get mad about another man pursuing his girlfriend? Why couldn't he be upset that she wanted another man? The urge to point out to him that this wasn't a 'business problem' that would resolve itself with proper consideration and planning danced on her tightly-leashed tongue.

Why can't you be more like Michael?

She winced at that. It was the last thing she wanted him to be. Wasn't it? Of course, it was. It had to be.

Josh took the glass from her hand and set both on coasters on the coffee table. He turned to her, his body crowding hers. Grace gasped, suddenly certain that they'd be eating Pietro's in the sated afterglow of hot sex.

As if intent on proving her right, he pressed her back into the arm of the couch, his mouth covering then parting hers, delving inside. She closed her eyes on a groan of delight. Grace turned slightly beneath him, winding her fingers in the waves at the back of his scalp, pressing her aching breasts to the hard lines of his chest. His fingers played at her nipple, causing both of them to tighten more forcefully.

The rest of the afternoon played out in her imagination, a montage of images: Josh pulling off her clothes and dropping them to the floor...then his own, his hands and mouth roaming her body, his length sliding home as she shattered around him...the living room, the bedroom, the shower.

His mouth left hers, and she moaned in protest, her hands sliding to his shoulders as he backed away.

"This is why you want him. This is what you miss."

Grace forced her eyes open, watching in dismay as he smoothed his hair, seemingly as discomfited as always with her mussing him...or her being particularly mussed.

"Josh," she began.

"This isn't me, Grace. This is him...Justice. But, this is what you want. I suspected it when you kissed me at Le Artiste. You've never kissed me that way, but I've never encouraged it."

She shook her head, squelching the mad urge to suggest that there was nothing wrong with a varied sex life.

Is that what you want? A safe guy and hot sex in the same package?

Well, what was wrong with that? Of course, this was the wrong time to point it out to Josh. There was simply no way to say it that wouldn't validate what he believed, and he believed...

Oh hell, I am projecting Michael onto him.

But, was it so impossible for him to occasionally get down and dirty, hot and sweaty about the whole thing?

As if he knew precisely what she was thinking, Josh drew her hand to his half-erect cock. "It really doesn't do it for me, Grace. I'm sorry."

"No need to be," she managed, straightening her skirt self-consciously and avoiding his eyes.

There wasn't. She'd known Josh's tastes fairly soon after she started seeing him. He was a fan of long, slow seductions. It wasn't that Grace didn't like the effects. On the contrary, Josh patiently brought her to multiple mini-orgasms many nights, finding his own only when she was sated.

But, he was also right. She wanted unrestrained sex. She wanted an explosive encounter—at least once in a while. In six months, she hadn't admitted it...even to herself, but what Josh offered wasn't enough.

"You're going to leave, aren't you?" he asked quietly.

"It's not what you think. I'm not going to Michael. He's not right for me."

The backs of his fingers feathered along the line of her jaw. "Neither am I. I wish I could be, but I can't. I hope you find what you need."

She nodded, pulling off the ring and offering it back.

Josh screwed up his face. "What is that thing, anyway?"

"You mean— If it's not from you, who is it from?" The etching was lovely, and she'd convinced herself that Josh had picked it up on a lark, but if it wasn't him...

"It's tacky enough to be from Justice," he noted in distaste.

Grace slid it back on her finger with a nervous laugh, unwilling to admit how much she liked it, in light of that comment. Even if they were through, Josh was a deep-pocketed client.

"No. If anything, it's from my sister, Valerie. It's just her quirky style." It really was more like Val than Josh, and Val might have been teasing her by using her full name on the packaging. Since there had been no return address, it could have come from anywhere.

A knock came at the door, and Josh straightened his shirt before heading to answer it. He looked back in surprise, as she opened the closet and retrieved her jacket.

"You're sure you won't stay for lunch?" he offered.

She managed a stiff smile. "I don't think that would be a good idea, Josh."

"Then grab my coat. I'll drop you at the gallery with your lunch. You probably have a lot of work to do for the tea." He opened the door and took the receipt from the delivery girl, signing it in his neat, compact script.

A peculiar pull at her heartstrings made her hesitate. Josh was perfect...or nearly so. It really was too bad that it was ending. "I can take a taxi. Anne can meet me outside with my purse."

He handed the receipt back then the pen. "Grace—"

"Your lunch will be stone cold before you get back here," she reasoned. It was bad enough that she was leaving the man, because he wasn't hot enough for her in bed; she wasn't going to make him eat a cold lunch on top of it.

He chuckled. "My usual is..."

"Honey roasted chicken on a bed of Caesar greens," she finished for him. How could she forget?

Josh closed the door and turned, food in hand. "Let me put mine away in the fridge, and I'll drive you back." He said it as if it were a foregone conclusion that he'd be driving her. Josh was often like that.

"Sure," she managed.

The trip back was as quiet as the trip out had been, yet somehow more peaceful. At the gallery, she reached for the door handle, unable to find the words to end it formally.

Josh turned her face back to his gently, placing a slow, solemn kiss on her lips. Grace participated fully, recognizing a last kiss much better when it came from a man who did things in an orderly fashion.

"Call me if you need me," he offered.

He didn't need to say more than that. They'd been friends before they were lovers. They could still be friends now that they weren't. Josh was like that.

"Thanks, Josh. You'll be at the Gemstone Tea. Won't you?"

"Of course." He smiled. "I always attend your shows. You know that."

Strange, Grace mused as she left his car behind, *how painless ending so intimate a relationship was*. Her break-up with Michael had been excruciating. Then again, she'd chosen Josh for one reason. From the beginning, she'd known he wouldn't break her heart.

Chapter Four

December 9

"Ready to go?" Anne asked.

Grace smiled, smoothing the ankle-length burnout black lace dress she'd chosen for this evening's festivities. She strolled into the front gallery, nodding to the serving crew. It was show time. Moments like this were what she lived for, what she worked until she couldn't see straight for. A Le Artiste show was guaranteed perfection.

The critics and patrons arrived, as usual, fashionably late. Though she was at the front door to greet them right on time, it was a full fifteen minutes before anyone but her staff and a few of the more eager artists arrived.

Josh was the fourth person through the door, laying a kiss on her cheek and complimenting her dress before he moved away to examine the exhibits...and probably choose a few to give as Christmas presents.

After that, it was one handshake and kissed cheek after another. A half an hour in, they were coming in droves, a sure sign of a successful show. In fact, Grace greeted so many people in the space of five minutes that she didn't notice the odd grip on her hand as she noted the *Herald* critic arriving until it was raised to a pair of warm, soft lips.

She snapped a look at the man, expecting it to be one of their older, European-born patrons, no doubt hurt that she hadn't welcomed him earlier. Her eyes locked with Michael's, her heart taking up a frantic rhythm. He laid a second kiss on her hand, his questioning gaze flicking down then up again.

Grace forced her smile not to falter, blushing as the camera flashed. "Welcome back to Le Artiste, Mr. Justice. I hope you have an enjoyable evening." She prayed he'd move on quickly.

He didn't. "How could I not when I'm here with you?" His voice was smooth and knowing.

Constructing a coherent sentence suddenly seemed a physical impossibility.

"You're beautiful," he whispered, leaning close to place a kiss on her cheek.

Grace looked toward the door self-consciously as it opened again, acutely aware of the warmth of his hand enfolding hers, the reaction of her body to his proximity and the cameras still flashing.

"I have people waiting," she breathed. "I should welcome them."

"Of course." Michael released her hand immediately, moving away into the crowd.

She placed her hand in the next patron's, leaning to kiss sweet old Mr. Alastor on the cheek. Grace faltered at the residual red of the stone, completing the kiss stiffly, trying to put the mocking color out of her mind as she continued greeting the guests.

The ring is wrong! Arousal, yes, but I cannot love Michael Justice.

* * * *

Michael snagged a flute of champagne, his heart

beating double time in pure joy. *Love! She loves me!*

When the stone turned that gorgeous shade of red, the urge to kiss her had been nearly maddening, but Michael wasn't that stupid. Even if Grace loved him— *And, she does!*—she wasn't ready to forgive him yet, and he couldn't blame her for that.

He sipped the champagne again, peeking at Grace as she pointed a critic to one of the glass display cases. She glanced toward her hand, seemingly disconcerted, and he prayed that she'd looked at it just after he'd left her.

That was the point, after all. Grace wouldn't give him another chance easily. Michael needed every ounce of luck and support he could get.

He turned back to the case in front of him, not truly taking in the art, considering how to proceed. This entire thing was so tenuous, so delicate that there really was no master plan. Every step was like walking further out onto a tightrope.

"That was in poor taste, Justice," a man's voice informed him. "Then again, I've come to expect it from you."

Michael didn't need to look over his shoulder to recognize Josh Winters. "I think the champagne is rather good. Do you suggest the white wine instead? Or perhaps the red? I admit I'm not particularly fond of red wine."

"I meant coming here."

"Ah. I see. Forgive me, Winters, but didn't you suggest I mingle with patrons?" He knew he was antagonizing Winters, but that was sure to happen eventually. After all, Michael wasn't walking away until he walked away with Grace. *Unless...*

No, he wouldn't consider the possibility of failure. Failure was not an option. He would get Grace back, and Winters wasn't going to be happy about it. What man wouldn't be enraged at the idea of losing her?

"I meant at your own showing," he growled.

Michael sipped the champagne, biting back a smile rather unsuccessfully. "You'll have to be more specific in the future. With my...appalling lack of people skills, I misunderstood you."

"Amusing." He didn't sound amused. Winters edged up and around so that he was facing Michael. "Stop playing games with Grace," he warned in little more than a whisper. "She doesn't want you."

"Then she can tell me. Grace is an adult and quite capable of—"

"She told me!" His blue eyes blazed in fury.

Michael's stomach tightened painfully. Though the ring wasn't wrong, Grace could forsake her true feelings. He'd never considered that. He'd foolishly assumed she'd follow her heart as she always had.

Until I broke it. What would he do if she refused him when he knew that she loved him? Like everything else about this mess, he'd have to play it by ear, if it happened.

"I won't let you break her heart again," Winters warned.

"I don't intend on it." *This time, I'm playing for keeps.*

* * * *

December 10

Grace stretched in bed, warm and comfortable. The Gemstone Tea had been the smash of the season. The gallery had filled with patrons and press until it had fairly burst at the seams, and though the final sales wouldn't be tallied until today, she felt certain that they'd broken their own record.

She went about her morning routine in an unhurried fashion. Anne would expect her to be a little late today, so there was no rush. She strolled into Le Artiste an hour late, her smile not dimmed in the least, feeling on top of the world, coffee in hand—and stopped cold.

Anne and Elizabeth looked up from a newspaper spread out before them, wide-eyed and blushing. A dozen different scenarios, each more disturbing than the last, passed through her mind.

"The critics panned us?" she asked woodenly. It seemed ludicrous when there was nothing but praise for them the night before, but it was the worst-case scenario. If that wasn't the case, she could deal with whatever was wrong.

"No!" they practically shouted together. Anne and Elizabeth dug through the pile of papers, handing her the three columns she'd been expecting.

Grace set her coffee and purse on the countertop, taking them and scanning them quickly. "Stunning collection of... The best in stone art... Precious, even the semi-precious... A stellar event..." She looked up in confusion. "I don't understand."

It was only then that she noticed her employees trying to ease more newspaper over the top spread.

She put out her hand, fighting back annoyance. "Give it."

Elizabeth turned a vivid red. "You don't want to—"

"It's just a gossip column," Anne cut her off with a sigh, "and I imagine someone is going to mention it eventually. I was just hoping that you wouldn't see it this morning, when... Well, when you're in such a good mood."

A lead weight seemed to sink her stomach to her knees. This wasn't happening to her. "Hand it over."

Anne did so with a resigned nod.

The photos caught her eye first. Grace swallowed a cry of disbelief at the picture of her and Michael, face to face with her hand enfolded in his. She glanced at the other two photos, wincing as she read the captions beneath them.

It was a timeline. The first picture was one of Michael planting an impetuous kiss on her lips at his first showing at Le Artiste, captioned "Diamond in the rough." The second was a picture of her greeting guests at a Lisa Renauld showing the month Michael left her, captioned "Lady loses her luster." The final caption made her groan aloud.

"Gemstone Tea. Romancing the stone."

"Grace..."

She waved Anne silent, reading the column in numb disbelief.

Artist Michael Justice is back in town, and sources say he's the reason for the renewed twinkle in gallery owner Grace Mallory's eyes. It's not dollar signs from her successful Gemstone Tea the young entrepreneur is seeing or even future revenues, though Mr. Justice is undeniably an earner for whatever gallery he shows in, and he reportedly has another show at Le Artiste next month. Word around town is that we'll be seeing a lot more of this couple...

"God, no," she pleaded. "How could she?" But, she didn't really have to ask that question. Josh's cousin had never cared for Grace, and with the break-up, Amelia would have seized at any opportunity to do something like this.

"Grace, calm down. You know you can't respond to this," Anne reasoned.

"I know." Anything she said to refute the column would be twisted, and the gossip mongers would be all over her until they got more to print.

And they will! She didn't question that Michael would try something like this again. Nor did she question that it would be as hard to ignore him as it had been at the tea.

Hard? Impossible!

The phone rang, and Grace scooped it up without taking her eyes off of the column. "Le Artiste," she answered automatically.

"Grace?" Michael sounded nervous, as well he should after pulling a stunt like this. "I don't know if you've seen the *Trib* yet, but—"

"I suppose you're happy. Nice bit of publicity for the playboy artist," she spat at him. This was all his fault, after all. Why shouldn't she be angry with him?

"I didn't plan this," he protested.

"You didn't plan to kiss my hand?"

"Well, of course I did, but I'm not the only man who kisses your hand or cheek, you know."

"This is your last show at Le Artiste, Michael." Tears stung at her eyes, and she blinked them away.

Damn him! He shouldn't be allowed to hurt her. Wasn't there something in the laws of break-ups that said that?

"You don't want that," he whispered.

"I have to..." She cleared her throat, abruptly aware of the feeling of it closing on her, cutting off her air.

"I'm sure your boyfriend will be overjoyed," he grumbled.

Grace didn't bother to correct him. She'd stopped living her life to stroke Michael Justice's ego long ago. Knowing she wasn't with Josh anymore would only spur him on.

"Grace—"

"I will see you on the twentieth to preview the paintings for your show. I will host the show. Other than that, you will deal with Anne. Am I understood?"

* * * *

Michael fisted the receiver in his hand, trying to force himself to speak when he wanted to scream in frustration.

"I said, am I—"

"Yes. I understand you."

"Then we have nothing more to say to each other."

She disconnected, surprisingly not by slamming the phone down in his ear. Michael stood there, heartsick, unable to conceive of what he'd do now. When the annoying tone announcing an open line started, he managed to hang up at last.

The damned gossip columnist had pushed her too far. He shouldn't have touched her in public, though he ached to do it. He should have found a way to touch her in private.

How? When? He'd taken the opportunity, because she'd been distracted by the event. But, the damn press had... He wanted to throttle...

Michael stormed to the table, grasped the paper, and scanned for the columnist's name. He stopped cold, fisting the paper in fury. "A.W. Winters. I should have known." Not Josh, but likely a close relative of his. It wouldn't have been hard for him to ask a favor to put Michael in the doghouse.

The mad urge to redecorate Mr. Winters' face settled in his mind, and he fisted his other hand in sympathetic preparation. Michael eased back to rationality slowly. That would just make things worse with Grace.

A smile flirted with his lips. Of course, if Grace read the columnist's name as he had, it would put good old Josh in the hot seat with her. That would be good.

He dropped the crumpled paper back on the table and strode across the room, barefoot and nude save the sweat pants riding low on his hips. There were only ten days until the preview, and Michael was determined that his latest piece would be ready in time.

* * * *

Grace's gaze strayed to the column again, much as they strayed to the mood ring. What was it about the scene that she couldn't seem to shake?

From years of dealing in art, she recognized the "frozen moment" sensation of the picture. It was a look that was impossible to duplicate with models, captured or lost forever.

His hand cradled hers gently, his lips poised as if to kiss again. She sighed at the memory, wondering when the photographer got this shot. Was it in that instant between the two kisses? She tilted her head, examining Michael's face. His eyes were focused downward, not meeting hers. It was the instant just after he'd kissed her hand the second time.

But, what was he looking at? Not her chest at that angle, though he had been rather fond of her chest when they were lovers.

She set her chin on one fist and traced his line of sight with the opposite fingernails. Her blood ran cold. "Son of a bitch!" It wasn't possible!

But, there was the proof. Michael was looking straight at the mood ring.

Grace fought for a coherent thought strand. He couldn't know what it was.

Unless he saw it change.

He would think it was a novelty piece. It was a Gemstone Tea, after all. He couldn't possibly know the color key for it, even if he thought it was a novelty.

Unless he bought it.

In her office, when he showed up to book the show, hadn't he glanced at her hands on the desk several times?

Usually just before he called me a liar.

The ring had arrived the same day he contacted her for the first time.

"It's tacky enough to be from Justice."

No. It was just a coincidence. Valerie must have sent it. It was just her sister's quirky style. Where was she now, anyway? Central America somewhere?

If Michael sent it...

"He didn't," she assured herself. "I just have to e-mail Val and thank her for the ring."

That would settle it—once Val wrote back. God only knew how long that would take, but surely she'd have an answer before Michael's show. In the meantime, it was time to get back to work.

Chapter Five

December 20

Grace sighed, as Michael wheeled the last of the crates in from his rented truck. He met her eyes, looking drawn and tense.

"Do you need my help to uncrate?" she asked, hoping he'd turn down her offer of aid.

A look of near panic flitted across his face then was gone. "No. I'll be fine. Maybe..." He looked at the crates nervously. "I'll set them out then call for you. Would that be all right?"

She stared at him, stunned by his response. "Yes, I suppose— I mean... Of course, it is."

He sighed as if in relief. "Good." Michael made no move to open the crates, watching her intently until she'd closed herself in her office. The sound of hinges creaking and paper rustling followed almost immediately on the click of the door lock.

Grace let out a shaky breath, willing the tension in her muscles to ease. She looked around her office, mentally searching for something to do. Work would be a lost cause. Until Michael left for the evening, there was little chance she'd be able to concentrate.

Her gaze settled on her computer, and she headed for the desk. Checking e-mail was the perfect way to waste time.

There wasn't much in there, though she hadn't had a chance to check it for the last two days. After she'd deleted a Nigerian scam that claimed she'd inherited five million dollars, a PayPal spoof claiming she had to update her credit card information, and three pieces of spam, there was only a shipping notification from FedEx—on a package she'd received that morning, an invitation to an art exhibition and auction for charity...and an e-mail from Valerie.

Grace hesitated, looking at the closed door between her and Michael nervously. She should open the letter and be done with it, but she didn't.

Why? her mind raged at her.

Opening it meant that she didn't trust him.

I don't trust him! I have no reason to trust him.

Then why did the thought of opening the e-mail make her heart ache?

Because I know what I'll learn. Then what will I do? How will I pull off his show if I find out he's done this?

But, she didn't know. Not for sure, anyway. *I should open it.*

Don't open it. Ask him.

Grace shook her head, trying to dislodge that idea, but it stuck. It made a certain amount of sense. She'd ask him, and she'd have Valerie's e-mail for proof of whether or not he lied to her. It was so crazy, it actually sounded sane to her.

Her legs shook lightly as she made her way to the door. She opened it, pausing while she took a calming breath. "Michael?" she called out.

He strode into view, looking back at the front gallery as if assuring himself that she couldn't see any of the paintings. She noted that uneasily. What was it about his work that unnerved him so badly? He'd had half a dozen showings, and she'd never seen him nervous before.

When she didn't speak immediately, he managed a rather tense, "Yes?"

"You..." She faltered. It was going to sound insane.

"Grace? What's wrong?"

She twisted the ring on her finger, and Michael locked on the movement. That made asking easier.

"You sent me this. Didn't you?"

He rubbed his fingertips over his eyes, grimacing.

"Michael?"

He met her eyes, nodding, looking like a child caught with one hand in the cookie jar. "Yes. The ring is from me."

Grace stared at him, her emotions warring within her. Part of her wanted to laugh. Part of her wanted to scream, cry, throw him out of her life—and still she ached at the thought of doing it.

Michael dropped his gaze from her face to the damned ring. The feeling of being spied on was too much. Grace pulled it off and threw it at him, turning on her heel and walking away.

"Wait, Grace," he pleaded.

"You used that thing to spy on me," she shouted, her face burning in embarrassment. No, she wasn't just embarrassed. She was mortified, exposed, violated, furious! "You... Every step of the way, you used it to set me up."

"That was never my intent," he informed her calmly.

"Then what was?" This was one she just had to hear.

"I wanted *you* to see how you really felt. I hoped... I hoped you wouldn't fight me as much if you still..." He growled in seeming frustration and tried again. "Yes, I looked at the ring! When I saw you wearing it, I couldn't resist. It's sort of addictive."

"Yes, I know." How stupid was she? How naïve? She'd let a piece of metal and stone run her life.

"I had to know, Grace. Please, believe me when I tell you that I had to know."

"It was wrong," she lied. "The ring... It was wrong, you know."

Michael didn't answer immediately. "It's never wrong, and you know it. I'll bet you tried to prove it. I did, too."

No. It was never wrong. "Why?" she managed, pressing trembling fingers to her lips to keep from sobbing.

"Why... I'm sorry. I don't know what you're asking."

"Why did you have to know what I'm feeling? Why did you want me to know it?"

The silence stretched between them for a long moment. Michael sighed, and there were faint sounds of movement. Grace stiffened, but he didn't seem to be approaching her.

"Look at me, Grace." It was more a request than an order.

She turned, gasping in surprise at the sight of Michael slipping the ring on his pinky finger. Her protest stuck in her throat as the stone started flickering through several emotions: lavender longing, purple...and red love.

"The ring wasn't wrong. I was," he whispered. "I've hated myself for lying to you every day for the last year. I've hated myself for hurting you and—"

"Then why did you do it?" Grace wished her voice held contempt, bitterness, hate, but she was too tired and confused to feel any of it, and Michael was right; she'd never been a good liar, at least not when she was face to face with someone.

She couldn't seem to get a handle on what she *did* feel. Relief? Shock? Longing? An insane thought flitted in her mind before she brushed it away. Taking the ring back just to figure out how she felt about this situation would be completely over the top.

"I was afraid. No. I was more than afraid. I was a coward, and I was angry."

"Afraid of me? What? Did you think I was making too many demands on you?" She didn't need the ring to tell her that his comment made her angry.

How dare he! She'd never been the clingy type. When he'd asked for space, she'd given him space. She'd never even hinted at the possibility of getting married. In the last month they were together, she hadn't even ventured to his studio, because he'd said he needed time on a painting, and she hadn't wanted to disturb his 'artistic flow.'

"In order, yes and no." Michael sighed, the stone turning butter yellow in nervousness. "Let me show you the paintings. That will explain it better than I can."

When she didn't advance on him, he offered his hand. Grace forced her feet to move, half-stumbling to him, meeting his eyes as his hand closed on hers. For a moment, neither of them moved. It was if they'd stood like this a thousand times, as if she could mark the moment Michael would lose control and kiss her.

He didn't. Michael shook his head, backing away slowly though the ring glowed bright pink. "The paintings." His voice was rough, deep, ready.

Grace took a calming breath and followed him to the front gallery.

Michael led her to the closest piece, blocking her view when she tried to look around at the rest. "In order...please. I have to explain this rationally."

She nodded, looking from his face to the painting propped against the wall, her eyes widening. "My God! Michael, this is wonderful." It was nothing like his typical style. The colors were vibrant and alive, a near-breathing representation.

"Do you remember it?"

A fragment of a memory flashed before her then took shape. "Okimo."

"Yes. That was where it started."

"It?" she asked, confused. It had been a simple hiking trip up Mount Okimo in Vermont. They'd had a picnic dinner at the summit on one of the last warm days of fall then made love as the sun went down. It was the sunset view from Okimo he'd painted, every stone and tree awash in a curtain of gold and red.

"Come see the next."

Though she wanted to examine the sunset a bit longer, she nodded and followed him. There would be time to come back later.

"Oh, Michael," she managed, barely breathing. If possible, this painting was even more beautiful than the last.

"The little gazebo at Landing Park," he noted, squatting to run his fingers along the upper edge fondly. He stood again, stuffing his hands in his pockets.

"Yes, I know." She tried to look at the next picture, but he blocked her way again.

Michael took her hand and rubbed his thumb across her knuckles. "Before you see the next, let me show you something."

Grace nodded, confused by his secrecy.

He pulled an envelope of pictures from his back pocket, opened it, counted out four and handed them to her with a wince.

She fought the urge to do the same when she saw what was on them. The canvases were in his signature blues, browns and gray, but the quality was uneven and the hand stiff. "How—interesting." She peeked up, hoping she hadn't offended him.

A wry smile curved the hard line of his mouth only slightly. "You never were a good liar. They sucked, Grace. I know it...and now you know it."

She looked at the painting of Landing Park in dawning understanding. "You lost your usual style, didn't you? Oh, Michael... I'm so sorry." No wonder he left.

Then again... Examining the new style, she wasn't certain why she was apologizing. It was beautiful, but Michael had been an artist comfortable in his style. Maybe he wasn't comfortable in *this* style.

He stroked her cheek, shaking his head. "Don't be sorry. Just tell me the truth. Do you like the vibrant pieces?"

"Of course. They're stunning, powerful..."

An honest smile brought the light to his eyes. "Thank goodness you can't lie. I know you really like them."

Her heart ached. "But you don't," she guessed.

Michael ran his fingertips along the top edge of the canvas again. "I've come to like it," he commented. "I won't lie to you. I didn't, at first." He pulled his hand back, abruptly uncertain. "I have to unpack more paintings. Take your time looking at the next four, and please...stop at the far wall. I have more to explain."

"All right." Of course, she'd agree. She'd wanted to understand, and now that Michael was finally opening up to her, how could he think she'd refuse him?

"Promise me you'll take one painting at a time and not look ahead." His expression was heartbreakingly hopeful.

"You have my word."

He smiled and leaned forward to kiss her, stopping inches away as if reasoning that it would be a bad plan. Grace didn't give him time to pull back. She placed a quick kiss on his lips much like the one the photographer had caught on film at his first show.

Michael stared at her, swallowing hard, his breathing quick and uneven. "Grace..."

"Get unpacking before I kiss you again." She kept her tone light, though his expression made her want to do a lot more than kiss him.

Michael chuckled, turning on his heel and striding across the gallery, glancing back at her as if assuring himself that she wasn't a mirage.

Grace studied the next four paintings intently, examining the fine level of detail on the canvases while she dimly noted Michael working furiously. He completely unpacked the front gallery while she identified the river view from her apartment window, ice floes on the partially frozen river as seen from Riverside Park, the clearing at the castle hiking trails. He moved on to the other galleries, unpacking the blue room while she explored his depiction of the castle at its center...then the Rounde as she gaped in wonder at how vividly he'd captured the Winter Solstice celebration at America's Stonehenge in Salem, New Hampshire.

The paintings were beyond exquisite. She could stare at them all day and still find more to see. Grace wanted to move on, but she'd given her word to wait.

"Michael?" she called out.

He came back in, dusting his hands on his jeans. When he realized which painting she stood before, he winced. "Time for explanations, I see," he grumbled.

"You were afraid you'd lose your audience. Weren't you?" And, he might, but the audience he'd gain would be just as powerful and influential. Doors that had been closed to him would be opened now. Gallery owners who didn't like angst would love this.

Michael darkened. "A shitty reason to break your heart."

"Yes. It was. You should have told me."

He nodded. "I can't argue that."

"Why did you have me stop here?"

"You didn't look ahead?" he asked in disbelief.

"I promised I wouldn't," she reminded him in irritation.

He seemed to have trouble forcing himself to speak.

"Michael?"

"I painted those in hopes that I'd get it out of my system—like my personal Red Phase or something, but it didn't work that way." He pulled out the pictures again and handed her three more.

Grace bit her lip painfully. "Would you be offended if I said that these were awful? They're worse than the others."

Michael took them back without comment, placing them behind the short stack he still held. "They were."

He met her eyes, seemingly miserable. She glanced at the ring, confirming his state of mind. If Michael noticed the move, he gave no sign of it.

"I was wrong, Grace. I was horrible to you. Yes, I was desperate, but I know that's no excuse."

She couldn't find the words to answer him. What could she say in the face of such a heartfelt apology?

"I knew I made a mistake immediately. No! Mistake is too soft a word. Forgive me. Words aren't my strong suit. You know that. Let me show you."

"Sure." Maybe that's why he didn't want her to look ahead. Maybe these six were the only decent canvases he'd produced in the last year. No. That wasn't like Michael. If he brought a truck, he had a truckload of worthy canvases. The pictures told the tale of his failures.

He handed her more pictures, half-finished blues. "I couldn't concentrate. I could barely hold a brush. All I could think of was you."

"You seem to have gotten over that," she noted, well aware of the bitter bite in her voice.

Michael paled. He turned her and guided her to the next painting. "All I could think about was you," he repeated, his voice hoarse.

Grace stared at him in confusion, looking down at the canvas only when he motioned toward it. She fought for an unhampered breath, unable to think clearly. Her own face smiled back at her, the wind on Mount Okimo tangling her hair around her face, a coffee mug halfway to her lips.

"You painted me? A portrait of me?"

Michael drew her away from the painting gently, turning her face toward the next without comment.

The painted Grace lay out on the grass in Riverside Park, her legs crossed at the ankles, her arms folded beneath her head, staring at the clouds drifting past.

She went on to the next.

Grace handed a Frisbee back to a group of children at Winnekenni.

And another...

She did cartwheels in a sunny storm.

Grace moved from one painting to the next, reliving a dozen moments in their life together. She turned to him, searching for words in her muddled mind.

"All I could think of was you. Nothing else mattered." Michael took her hand and kissed it much as he had at the Gemstone Tea. He placed it on his arm and escorted her toward the blue room. "Come see the rest."

"Of me?" she asked. Surely, he couldn't have painted more of her.

"All I could—"

"Oh, Michael. You know... If I carry this show, I'll have to give you another chance. What would the gossip columnists and critics say about you painting me, if we weren't seeing each other? They'd say you were obsessed, psychotic..."

He smiled a near-predatory smile. Before she had a chance to question it, he'd motioned her to the first of the paintings in the blue room.

"Dear God!" No wonder he'd worried about her carrying more than the main body of work.

The portrait was one of her asleep in his sleigh

bed, her hair fanned over the empty pillow beside her, the sheets tangled around her body, thankfully covering the essential parts, one arm curled around her head while the other lay across her hips. She gasped in the realization that her nipples were beaded against the sheet.

"It's tasteful," he pointed out nervously. "A boudoir shot, more or less."

"You have more like this," she guessed.

Michael shot her a sidelong glance, nodding silently.

Grace moved from painting to painting without comment, evaluating each. He'd done one of her in a long silk robe, beckoning him into her bedroom. Another showed her wrapped in a bath sheet, her wet hair in long curls around her face. Another showed her sitting up in bed, one leg extended from under the sheet. Still another showed her in one of Michael's dress shirts, looking at him over her shoulder, a wicked smile on her pinked face.

The last made her head spin. "It's the night of the Gemstone Tea," she breathed. *From his point of view.* The portrait was from her chest up, the look of longing the camera had captured on her face, her hand clasped in Michael's, the only bit of him in the painting, and the ring shining red. He'd finished this in a little over a week?

His hands closed on her shoulders. "You were so beautiful, so enchanting, I couldn't help myself."

The double meaning hit her solidly, heating her blood for him. Maybe it was the wanton feeling of him touching her that sealed her decision. Either way, she didn't question it. "They can stay in the show." After all, they *were* no worse than boudoir shots.

Michael turned her toward him, looking stunned. He cupped her chin up and kissed her, slowly and completely, parting her lips with a groan. He broke away, his eyes still closed as if savoring her taste. "Thank you."

She didn't ask if he was thanking her for letting him show the portraits or for the kiss. At that particular moment, coherent thought seemed an odious chore. "We should— I should see the rest."

His eyes opened, and he cleared his throat, looking distinctly uncomfortable. "The...ah...rest of them won't be showing."

His meaning hit her full force. "You didn't!"

"Maybe I am just a little obsessed." His words had the sound of an apology.

Grace pushed past him and raced into the Rounde. The first portrait brought her up short, unable to form words, even an expletive.

It was a simple head and shoulder piece, unclothed, her head thrown back, hair mussed and eyes closed. Though there was no clear indicator of when he'd seen her like this—*Probably, many times!*—it was obvious that she was in the throes of passion.

"Are you furious?" Michael asked quietly.

She struggled for words, her unresponsive mouth staging a revolt against her disorganized mind. Grace grasped his hand with a growl of frustration, dragged the damned ring off of his finger and pushed it onto her own. If she couldn't tell him, she'd show him.

Michael stared at the rapidly-shifting colors, his lips moving silently, no doubt cataloging one chaotic emotion after another. "Not angry," he mused, "but you do need positive focus."

His meaning wasn't lost on her, though she couldn't seem to decide how she felt about it at first. The kiss started off a slow exploration, but this was Michael; it wouldn't remain that way for long. In moments, her hands were roaming his body, pushing up at his sweater, their mouths meshing passionately.

He pulled away, laboring breaths in and out. "Not yet."

Grace looked at him in shock. "I think that's the first time you've ever said that to me. No. I *know* that's the first time."

Michael darkened. "I've done a lot of things wrong, Grace. This won't be one of them."

"I don't understand." She didn't. He thought there was something wrong with the way they'd always made love? Based on the revelations of this evening, she was more convinced than ever that it was the single, purest part of their relationship.

He pulled the pins from her hair and combed his fingers through it. "*If* we're going to pursue this, we'll do it right. That means you breaking off things with Winters first."

She bit back a laugh, half at the stress he put on the word 'things' and half in his obvious attempt at chivalry.

"This isn't funny, Grace," he protested. "And, it's non-negotiable."

"Oh, but it is funny."

"I will not allow Josh Winters—or whoever...whatever Winters is the gossip columnist to say you were screwing around on him. It will be properly over before I take you to bed."

"Or to my desk?" she teased.

"Especially not to your desk!" He shifted uncomfortably, the bulge in his jeans no doubt pinched.

"Well... Then maybe you should take me to my desk...or to bed." She trailed her fingertips over the bulge, watching it harden further and wondering how long it would be until he couldn't stand her teasing anymore. "They won't be saying that."

"I'm serious, Grace." He gave up and adjusted the package so that it lay just behind the buttons on his jeans, straining them.

"So am I. We've been broken up for a month."

Michael went so absolutely still, a look of confusion on his face, she was certain he hadn't heard her and was trying to piece together what she'd said.

"I said—"

"I heard you. His idea or yours?"

"Mutual. We weren't right for each other. We make better friends than lovers. We both knew it."

"I'm..." He scowled.

"You're not sorry."

"No. I'm not." He sighed. "Now, I'm sorry. I told you words aren't my thing." Michael stroked his fingertips along the line of her jaw. "You're sure you want this? I can wait until you're ready."

"I think I've waited long enough." It seemed that she'd been waiting for this since the last night they spent together.

His smile sent shards of light through his eyes. "I'll pack the other two rooms, if you pack this one," he offered.

"Your place or mine?"

"Definitely mine."

Her heart skipped at that. *Of course, his. It's closer.* "Deal."

Michael laid a quick kiss on her lips and bolted away.

"Don't damage the canvases," she shouted after him.

"Never!"

Grace smiled, loading the portraits back into the crate, the erotic images making her arousal more than painfully clear to her. She paused with a truly wanton piece in her hands. The Grace on the canvas had half-covered her breast with splayed fingers so the erect nipple peaked through the gaps between. That breast fairly ached for attention. And, so did she...the *real* she.

She smiled, putting the rest of the paintings in the crate. This idea was too delicious to pass up.

Her blouse, bra, pantyhose and panties folded over the crate, she set the portrait against the far wall and sat next to it. Grace fluffed her hair and posed herself to her best advantage, one knee bent, the high heel flat on the floor, her skirt hiked nearly to the crease of her thigh to accomplish it. She draped her hand across her breast much as it was in the painting, smiling that her nipple was already erect just from the thought of what she was doing.

"Michael," she called out.

As he had the last few times, he came to her immediately—and went absolutely still in the doorway, his wide eyes tracing every line of her body.

"I thought you could use some inspiration," she purred.

"Is the gallery closed tomorrow?"

"You know it is." That's why she'd scheduled his viewing for tonight. "In fact, it's the start of Christmas vacation for the staff." No one except a daily security sweep would be here for the next two weeks. Had he forgotten the schedule she kept? "Why?"

"I'm *inspired* to keep you up all night." He pulled the buttons on his jeans open with one tug. "God knows I will be."

He scooped his sweater over his head and tossed it toward the crate, missing by several feet. She'd always wondered at how defined his chest and arms were, though she'd once joked with him that he kept his physique from sex more than from any other form of exercise.

Michael didn't spare the sweater any attention; he strode toward her, his eyes locked on hers. Grace found it hard to breathe. There was never any question that sex would be explosive when he had that focused look on his face.

He sank to his knees before her, trailing the fingertips of both hands up her inner thighs as he leaned forward and captured the nipple peeking from between her fingers in the heat of his mouth. The dull throbbing at the apex of her thighs spread outward and became a potent drumbeat of anticipation, punctuated by the flicks of his tongue and his insistent sucking. Michael moved from one nipple to the other, enflaming her with ruthless efficiency.

Grace grasped at his hair, matching his moan of pleasure at the move. His slowly-traveling fingers converged on their goal, one hand massaging her mound and clit slowly while the other breached her body.

That was her breaking point. She dragged his jeans halfway to his knees, stroking his cock, guiding him forward, demanding him silently.

Michael's mouth and hands left her and he rose up, cupping her buttocks and lifting her, holding Grace so that his cock brushed the sensitive skin he'd been massaging. "Are you going to come as fast as you did the first time, Grace?" he taunted, seating himself just inside her.

She shivered, immersed in the memories of him kissing her, taking down her hair...then her panties and thrusting inside her on her desk. "Faster," she panted, wrapping her hands over his shoulders and her legs around his waist.

"Mmmm. We'll see." He pulled her down over him, thrusting up at the same time so that his full length rammed home at once.

Grace screamed in delight, moving against his manic hip thrusts, arching her back as she shattered, her hands tightening on his shoulders reflexively.

"Too fast," he moaned, following her over, his ragged cry mixing with hers as the hot wash of his climax did the same.

For several long minutes, they stayed like that, curled together on the floor, their breathing slowing, their bodies entwined.

"I'm sorry I couldn't make it last longer that time," Michael offered. "First time overload, I guess."

Grace laughed.

"What is it?"

She laid a kiss on his chest. "Well, you did promise me all night. I figure the more times you push us both over that quickly, the more times we..."

Michael captured her mouth with a whispered curse.

Epilogue

January 14

"Michael," Grace warned, pushing his face away from her neck with a hearty flush. She waved him away. "You paint. I'll read."

He chuckled, glancing back at her as he walked away, noting her perusal of him instead of the newspaper in her hand in satisfaction.

She cleared her throat. "Sporting... Who says sporting, anyway? It sounds like I have a black eye."

"Grace," he warned. "I'm coming back there."

"You have a deadline."

"Slave driver," he muttered. But, she was right. The Cambridge show was only eight months away.

"I'll get my whip out later," she commented, obviously distracted.

"I could always show the exotics," he suggested, placing Vermillion on his palette.

"If you weren't painting..."

He smiled. "Read, woman!"

"Oh, yes. Sporting a small diamond ring... It's not small," she complained.

"She's a Winters," he sang back.

"That's true, and not a very nice one at that. How Josh got such a—"

"Grace."

"Okay. 'Grace Mallory, owner of Le Artiste Art Gallery on River Street, is back on the arm of Massachusetts' hottest homegrown artist, Michael

Justice. Is it wedding bells we're hearing, or will Haverhill's own Runaway Bride do it again?' That bitch! I have never broken an engagement before. In fact...I've never been engaged before."

Michael faltered in mixing coral, fighting back a shocked laugh. Amelia Winters hadn't let up on Grace since the night of the Gemstone Tea. Of course, the panties they'd forgotten in the Rounde at Christmas hadn't helped, though thankfully they'd removed the exotic paintings before the first security sweep.

He went back to his work. "Well, won't it be a disappointment to her when you don't?"

"I suppose."

"What else does she say?"

"The usual. Big city morals dragged to our fine burgh. Scandals waiting to break. My tacky ring that no one seems to be able to agree on the color of. Isn't it just a shame that the colors never photograph?" she noted sarcastically.

"Do you really like it that much?" he asked, scowling at the too dark mixture and evaluating its usefulness. Maybe for shadowing...

"I think we should get a more masculine one in the same style and both wear them."

"Why?"

"It would be hard to mis-communicate again when we can read each others' emotions."

"I suppose it would. Why not? The proceeds from one painting will cover the ring." *Even as expensive as the 'real, magical' mood rings are.*

It wouldn't be a hardship to buy it. Michael had sold sixteen of the twenty-six paintings he'd displayed at Le Artiste. The show had been dubbed the season's smash hit, and Michael Justice's new style was the talk of critics across New England.

Better, the ten remaining paintings and another six or eight would show in Cambridge in the fall. All Grace had to do was keep playing the part of muse. He flicked a glance at her, curled on his bed, the sheets pooled at her hips, nude otherwise. She inspired him in more ways than he could count.

Michael strode toward her, uncertain as to why the red on his palette resonated with him when it wasn't the color he'd intended on mixing. "Grace? What does this color remind you of?"

She studied the palette, her smile spreading and her blush deepening.

"Grace?"

She extended her right hand toward him, the stone in the mood ring a deep red that nearly matched what he'd mixed. "It's the color of love, Michael."

"Then, I'll use it in every painting," he vowed. "Just for you."

Overtime Pay

Evelyn Jacobs leaned across the rail, drinking in the night air, heavy in the scent of sea salt. It was a perfect night, one to make you want to climb on the rails and lean far out screaming, "I'm king of the world." Leo's character certainly knew what he was doing in that scene, she decided.

Phillip wrapped his arms around her waist, pulling her to the heat of his body. "Not too far," he teased.

The already-erect length of him pressed into the curve of her buttocks, announcing how much her short skirt excited him. If she leaned just a little further, they could give some topside sailor a hard-on with the show they would make.

"I like to go too far," she teased him, well aware that someday Phillip would take her up on that offer. The thought both excited and terrified her. It was all part of the game, the chance of being caught. She shivered in the imagined climax that would roll through her body if someone caught them in the heat of the moment.

"I know." His hand slid under her skirt, testing her readiness. "Very good. So ready for me." His voice was rough, a sure sign that there was more to this outing than teasing. He meant to follow through. As if confirming that, the whisper of a zipper sounded behind her.

They'd talked about using Velcro like strippers often did, but they abandoned the idea for two reasons. One was that the Velcro was actually louder than a

73

zipper. The other was that hint of danger. Velcro made it far too easy not to get caught. It was too quick.

"Here?" she asked breathlessly. "Now?" Her nerves tingled in the idea that Phillip had finally taken her up on the tease. Some lucky sailor was about to get a show that would send him to some equally lucky maid's bed that night.

"Soon." His fingers played inside her, announcing his impatience. "Five," he whispered. "Three. One."

Everything happened at once. The deck and rigging lights went out. Phillip leaned her over the rail and slid to the hilt in her. Evelyn gasped in surprise and delight, moving against his thrusts. He was always different at moments like this, not the gentle lover she often saw in the bedroom but ravenous sex unleashed.

"How long do we have?" she asked.

Phillip didn't pause, his body pistoning in hers, his heavy sac slapping against her with every forward thrust. "Three minutes."

Evelyn swallowed a scream of pleasure, as the shock pitched her over the edge. She almost laughed at that. Phillip knew what that announcement would do to her. He knew exactly how to play at her body and mind. Visions of the rigging lights coming up and sending him over into climax in the bright glow was too much for her.

He groaned as he joined her in climax, his hot come jetting into her, a flood of fluid that would coat her thighs on the way back to their room. When the door closed behind them, he'd ask to see it and take her again. Nights like this were always energetic ones sexually.

"God, that was good," he commented, as if Evelyn didn't know very well how much he enjoyed this particular form of torture.

He lingered inside her, and her body was wracked in aftershocks, wondering how close to the three-minute mark they were. It was delicious, not knowing whether or not the lights would come up before they were done. Then he was slipping free from her still-spasming body, easing her to her feet, smoothing her skirt over her rear.

Evelyn turned to him, kissing Phillip passionately as she tucked him inside his trousers and zipped them up. They'd managed to get away with it again.

The lights came up, and Phillip grinned. "Ten seconds early. We'll have to be faster at the pool."

* * * *

"I don't understand why that main breaker pops so often?" Jerry grumbled. "Once every run, it seems."

Alex smiled. It was the most popular spot, the most public for the couples who wanted to use it. "Which do you think will go next? The pool, the exercise room, or the restaurant?"

Jerry groaned. "Who cares. I'm just sick of this. When I signed on to this tub, we didn't have these problems."

"She was ten years younger then." And a good thing for Alex! This way, he could blame the problems on the age of The Mysterious. If she were a younger ship, three dozen maintenance men from the builder would be crawling all over her, trying to find the problems and screwing up his side business.

His boss ran his black-stained fingers through a shock of white hair, making it stand on end. Jerry was always like this when these unexplained blackouts struck The Mysterious. Alex was certain that the captain laid into Jerry about it, and that should make Alex feel at least a little guilty, but he managed to console himself that Jerry was pulling in the big bucks for sitting on his ass and sending Alex and Mack off to fix anything that went wrong. If the hardest things the old man did were changing a few bearings and taking heat from the captain, Alex couldn't feel all that sorry for causing the latter.

"If you don't need me anymore tonight," Alex hinted.

"No. Turn in, but be sure to hit that dishwasher in the main kitchen first thing tomorrow. I don't want to hear any more crap about that bitch not holding the proper one-ninety."

"You got it, boss."

Alex left Jerry's office, fuming at that order. Twice a week, he was given this duty. When Alex set the dishwasher temperature higher, the kitchen staff complained the water was scalding them through their protective clothing. When he set it just a notch lower, the old man complained that it was running just below the suggested one hundred and ninety degrees. You'd think two degrees would kill someone, the way they acted. Most land-based restaurants had their sanitizers set for one-eighty, but trying telling that to the fascist in charge of food service.

He reached his quarters in no time at all. Alex smiled at the two other empty racks. George worked night shift in the engine room, and Mack would be busy screwing Trudy in some dark corner for the next few hours. As always, this was his down time. He bolted the door.

Alex pulled the binoculars from his tool pouch, hooking them up to the computer and stripping off everything but his shorts while the file uploaded. Mack had Trudy, and Alex had this. There was one almost every trip, a rich man or woman with a taste for dangerous sex, the chance of discovery. They paid well, well enough to buy him this toy after only six runs, just a nice chunk of overtime pay.

The binoculars were state of the art, light gathering, digital video recording, like watching a movie filmed on a hazy afternoon instead of in the pitch black of a moonless night or the belowdecks. The only thing missing was the sound, but Alex could add his own sound easily enough, alone in his room, beating off to the sight of people fucking all over the ship.

He got to watch it while he taped them, of course, but Alex couldn't indulge himself properly then. There was always the chance of Mack or Jerry showing up. Hiding the binoculars was easy enough. Hiding his favorite pastime while he watched wouldn't be.

Alex lubed up with a little K-Y, the only thing for a truly smooth glide. He punched the button to start the playback, taking his already rigid cock in his hand.

He sighed, pumping his hand up and down in time with the good Mr. Jacobs' frantic thrusts into his pretty bride. Her face was a study in exquisite pleasure, and Alex groaned at that. It was always best when you could see the mixed fear and ecstasy on their faces.

His hand moved faster, as she reached her climax. Oh yeah. This one was good. He would blow with Jacobs. There was no doubt about it. Few of them were this good. Few of them were this hot, the ones who truly loved the game they played. These were the ones that made the boring, half-hearted, clumsy attempts he often saw worth it. This was almost worth more than the money.

The knock at the door sounded just as he would have come, and Alex cursed wildly at the poor timing. He turned off the monitor, letting the tape loop through. If it was Mack, he'd find a way to get rid of him quickly. One way or the other, Alex would finish what he started tonight. He pulled a robe over his shorts and wrenched the door open.

His heart stuttered. It wasn't Mack. It was Jacobs, looking far more pressed and polished than he had while he'd been thrusting into his lady. Alex glanced to the computer nervously, assuring himself that there was nothing for the other man to see.

"Alex," he rumbled. "May I come in?"

"Uh. If you want to cancel the rest of the nights—or change one, just let me know," he managed in an even tone.

"May I come in?" he repeated patiently.

"Sure." Alex moved back and waved him inside.

Jacobs strode in, his hands shoved in his pockets, his eyes surveying the cramped room. He picked up the binoculars, his eyebrow rising in surprise. "Nice setup. Light gathering and recording. What's your capacity? Forty meg?"

"Eighty. The new chip."

"But, no sound. Too bad. I saw one on shore today with a detachable wireless mic."

Alex swallowed hard, trying to figure out Jacobs' game. Was the man upset that he'd watched them? Did he even know for sure?

As if answering that question, Jacobs put down the binoculars and turned the monitor on. He whistled a long, low note then looked to Alex's state of undress pointedly. "Having fun?"

This was it, the literal end. If Jacobs went to the old man—or the captain about this— Hell, he could even admit paying Alex off at this point, and the blame would still fall on Alex. "Look, man. I didn't mean any harm."

"I asked if you were enjoying yourself." He looked back to the screen. "She is sublime when she comes," he whispered.

"What is it you want, Jacobs?" The waiting was killing him. Alex had to know what the other man had in mind.

His eyes were like chips of blue ice. "We need to talk."

* * * *

"Hmm," Evelyn purred. "And what brought this on?"

Phillip smiled at that. He was fired up tonight, and she could sense it in his aggressive attitude. "I want to reward you for a fabulous trip."

"The offer of taking me again at Christmas isn't enough reward?" She sighed, as he pulled the panties off of her ankles and tossed them away.

He pushed her skirt up and dragged her to the edge of the sofa, earning him a look of pleased surprise. "For tonight, I want you to sit back and watch the DVD of our trip while I relax you."

Evelyn smiled at that. "Relax me? I hardly think relaxed is what you want from me."

"If you find yourself inspired," he teased.

"Start the video."

Phillip started the video, setting the remote next to her hip. He waited long enough to motion her eyes to the screen before he lowered his tongue to her clit, tilting his head to her thigh to watch her while he played. Evelyn sucked in her breath, her eyes darting between the screen and his face.

"The screen," he ordered.

She complied, fisting her hands in the skirt bunched high on her thighs. Phillip smiled at that. She'd read his mood correctly. He was in charge as he was when they played in public. Evelyn wouldn't dare touch him without his consent, though she ached to do it.

He licked at her clit, rolling his tongue in circles that were sure to drive her crazy while he eased two fingers into her. Evelyn jumped at that then groaned. Her eyes flicked to him again, then returned to the screen, knowing he would stop to order it if she didn't do so of her own accord.

On the screen, Evelyn romped in the waves, her laughter high and clear. Phillip played at her body more urgently, wanting her at the edges of climax when his surprise played out.

Right on cue, Evelyn tensed, crying out harshly as the scene changed. Phillip thrust his tongue into her, groaning at the changing taste of her body and her inner muscles contracting around his invading tongue, sucking at him gently.

The sound from the speakers stopped, silenced by her jab at the remote. "How?" Her voice was full of wonder at that, as if he'd just given her the most fantastic gift, just as he'd hoped it would be.

Phillip kissed her clit, chuckling as she shivered in response. "Our electrician friend had a sideline."

"He offers this?"

"He does now that I've upgraded his equipment a bit. I thought he might be up to something when the lights came up early that first time. When I learned I was right, I made a deal with him to record the rest of our planned encounters." Phillip noted her curving lips. "You're not really upset, are you?"

She laughed. "Of course not. I've been teasing you with getting caught for a long time."

"Good."

Evelyn met his eyes, furrowing her brow at that. "Why? Because you have them all on DVD?"

"No. Because, I intend to do it again."

"Again?"

"You will never know when our friend is watching and when he isn't. His layovers in town are at odd intervals."

She gasped at that, her color rising. "Oh, Phillip."

"Would you like that?"

Her nod was slow and shaky, her eyes locked on the image of them on the screen.

* * * *

"God damn this," Jerry thundered. "It's worse than ever. Consistently three times a trip, at least. The company is threatening to close this tub down."

"They wouldn't really decom The Mysterious. Would they?"

For the first time, Alex felt a pang of fear. Sure, he'd still have the Jacobs, and that wasn't chump change, but any other ship in the Mystic Fleet would be far too new for him to do this on. Not to mention, it would become apparent that the problems followed Alex, if anyone cared to check up on things like that.

Jerry shook his head. "Naw," he sighed. "Our jobs are safe, such as they are. As long as we can keep this tub running, she'll stay in service. There seem to be a lot of people who request her. No idea why. You'd think they'd want to have the new ships with all the special features, but they want this old beast. I will never understand it."

Alex smiled. *No. You never will.*

May the Best Man Win

Prologue

A future not so far away

June 19th

"You just had to say it," Bainbridge Carter grumbled, shouldering David up. He ran for the waiting truck, sliding in the mud-filled gouges in the abandoned logging road. He rounded the body of the downed Federalist soldier with a sneer of disgust. Killing your former brothers-in-arms got a hell of a lot easier when you saw that uniform, he decided.

David Evans barked a harsh laugh, stumbling along. It was a half-mad sound Bain had heard from him many times, usually before or just after David did something insanely stupid. Only this time, he hadn't decided to balcony-dive into a hotel pool or surf in the back of a moving pick-up truck. This time, the damned fool had gotten himself shot.

"Chief Carter!"

He looked up at Samuels, shaking his head, at a loss for words. Bain hefted David into the back and scrambled up after him. Samuels shut them in, then jumped in the front and started them rolling, into the trees and toward safe territory.

As if anywhere is safe, these days.

The time to think about the war was later. They had more immediate problems, most of them caused by the illustrious David Evans.

Bain didn't waste time. He dragged David's shirt open, his jaw tensing at the damage beneath. "You fucking idiot," he whispered.

All David had to do was stay cool for two more minutes, and he would have survived. But David had always been about immediate gratification, impatience at its finest.

"Knew it would end this way," David rasped. He waved off Bain's move toward the medical kit. "Save it for someone who needs it. I'm done."

Bain nodded, settling into the shifting and swaying bed of the truck again. There was no saving David now, and they both knew it. Disconcerted, he pulled the rifle from his back and examined it.

All of this for a new weapon, one that would at least win them a stalemate, a solid line of defense in this insane conflict. He glanced at David out of the corner of his eye and away again, wondering, not for the first time, if any of it would be worth it in the end.

He fingered the gap in the stock in sick resignation. The specs said the control unit locked in place. He couldn't have dropped it. They couldn't have left it behind. His blood ran cold in the certainty that there was something very wrong here.

"Where's the control unit, David?" The rifle was useless without it, this entire set-up wasted.

David laughed harshly. He coughed, then panted in response to the pain. He pulled the unit from his pants pocket with blood-streaked fingers, passing it over.

Bain took it, his mind working hard at David's game. He met his former friend's eyes. "They would have found it," he mused. "Why would you remove..." Bain rolled the block of plastic in his hand, his mind kicking into high gear. "Something missing, David?"

David's smile was brittle and smacking of sarcasm. "Always were smart, weren't you, Bain?"

Not smart enough. That truth still stung.

"The chips..." He grimaced at a particularly bad bump on the logging road. "Accelerometer and gyroscope."

"Where are they?" Damn David's games! There was too much riding on this to play games. The lines wouldn't hold forever. They needed a superior weapon, not to advance but to hold the ground more effectively.

A tear welled up at the corner of David's eye. "I gave them to *her.*"

Bain's heart pounded, and his mouth went dry. *Ari.* He'd wondered if he'd see her again when David contacted them. Her absence, when he'd reached the rendezvous point, had been both a relief and a disappointment.

"I hid them," David continued. "I told her...never to let them out of her sight."

Fury rose up, hard and fast.

Bain wanted to shake David until he killed what was left of his damned mind. "How could you?" he raged. There was too much at stake for this insanity.

"Now you have an incentive," David spat.

For Ari, I would have an incentive, anyway. Obviously, David had taken Bain's capitulation all those years ago for a loss of interest. "Where is she?" he managed evenly.

"They. It's a package deal, Bainbridge."

He nodded his understanding. David had always been more concerned about Lea than he'd been about Ari.

"On their way to Blue Top."

Bain's heart stuttered. "You sent her to Blue Top? Along the refugee trail? Into the middle of that mess? What were you thinking?" Had he ever thought something through...in his entire life?

"I didn't know." Misery made David appear decades older than he had moments before. "At the time... I didn't know what was brewing at Blue Top." The tear slid down David's cheekbone to his ear. "Promise me, Bain. I want to hear it."

He nodded, his breathing strangled. "If she's alive"

David glared at him.

"If they're alive," Bain amended, "I'll find them, David."

"They're alive." David's eyes slid shut. "They're alive. She'll take care of Lea for me. Make her promise."

Bain nodded, only marginally aware that David couldn't see it, his mind racing from one thought to the next.

Why would Ari have to promise that? Her caring for Lea was a given. Ari doted on her daughter...at least, she had the last time Bain saw them.

How am I supposed to find them in the center of hell? Any attempt at reaching the refugee camps that had formed in the mountains would have to come from the north and by land instead of air. *A hell that's frozen over for most of the year.*

Most of all, he wondered what would happen when he came face to face with Aurora Evans again. They

86

hadn't parted on the best of terms. She'd made her choice, a choice Bain still couldn't understand, and the lesser man had taken the prize.

It was hours later, after Bain had turned David's body over, sometime during the debriefing, when Bain realized David had never once said his wife's name.

Chapter One

August 26th

"With all due respect–" Bain began.

"I seriously doubt respect is high on your list of priorities, Carter," Captain Elias replied dryly.

Bain ground his teeth at the delay.

"I know you think finding them is important." Elias waved Bain off before he could offer a retort to that. "And it may be, but right now we have a mission to attend do. After that..." He sighed. "After that, find her, if she's still alive."

That last comment was half-swallowed, a sure indicator that Elias, like most of the others, believed Ari was dead.

"She's alive," Bain attested. He didn't question that it was so. Ari wasn't the type to give up and die.

But she could be killed. The people at the camp were killed.

Unbidden, the carnage they found at Refugee Ridge filled his mind. The massacre had been a driving force in unifying the Free Nationalist troops. "Remember Refugee Ridge" was more than a cute alliteration.

Their initial spate of fury and outrage had won them the most decisive victories in the war so far, but it hadn't saved the people the Federalist bastards had wiped out. It hadn't produced Ari. It had left them, some of the less battle-hardened crying over the dead, in the ghost of a refugee camp, with more questions than answers, the two Bain sought conspicuously missing.

Bain pushed that thought away. Ari's van might have been at the camp, but her body...and Lea's body hadn't been. Barring the remote possibility that the Federalists knew what David hid with them and were looking for it, too, the possibility that they'd captured both Ari and Lea alive, the two were still on the run in the mountains.

Ari was resourceful. The fact that there were bags of flour, sugar, and rice stacked on cases of canned goods in the back of her van, didn't mean she was without food. The fact that there were boxes and bags of clothing and camping gear in it didn't mean she was without shelter and clothing. He'd seen how she packed a sea bag.

Elias's voice brought him back to the discussion.

"Now...about the current problem."

"Father Hubbard, huh? Someone was bored, when that one was coined."

"Well, he *is* traveling with about a half dozen kids."

"About? Usually, we know what we're dealing with." *Usually, I know why I'm being sent out on this sort of mission.* Bain was an electrician, not a Seabee or a S.E.A.L....or engineering or special forces of any other branch. If he was being sent out, it usually meant they needed the trust of someone he already knew. *Like David.*

Elias smiled, an odd expression for him these days. "This one's smart. They hide during the day and travel at night. The only surveillance we've gotten has been dark and..." His smile disappeared.

"And?" Bain questioned, his interest piqued.

"Whoever he is, he's good at hiding his identity, but we think he's one of ours."

Bain straightened. Another trained man was good news. *If it's true.* "Which branch? Navy?" Not that it mattered these days. A military man of any sort was as good as any other. But, if he was Navy, it would explain why they wanted Bain to go out there.

Elias nodded. "Navy, if we're right. He's wearing a pea coat and what looks like one of our ball caps...maybe submariner."

A close match for me. "Can't you make out the boat on the front?"

Elias shook his head. "Smudged. They think... They think it's a first class."

"Rate?" Bain didn't doubt that he wouldn't get an answer. If Elias knew the answer to that, he'd have said it already.

"Smudged out."

Bain nodded. "We'll have to take this one slow and easy." There was no guarantee that "'Father Hubbard" was on their side. There was no guarantee he was sane. What they'd find would be a crap shoot.

"Use caution, Carter."

"Don't I always?"

Bain grinned at Elias's scowl. How many times had Elias called him to the carpet for his lack of caution?

At least I'm not suicidal.

No. That had been David's game.

* * * *

August 29th

90

Aurora Evans wrung out the cloth, shuddering hard when the cool water touched her burning skin. Her eyes felt dry and gritty, and her head was in a flat spin. Her stomach roiled, and her eyes slipped shut. Though her entire body was quaking, she had to get on her feet in a couple of hours and lead the kids as far as they could trek tonight.

We're not going to make it.

Ari revised that thought guiltily. *I'm not going to make it.* She'd promised them they'd make it into safe territory, but her body was going to give out before she got them there.

I've done all I can. Ari had taught Lea to use the compass and maps. Her thirteen-year-old daughter was the oldest of the kids fate had left in her care. The rest were strays unlucky enough—or lucky enough, depending on your point of view—to be with Ari and Lea when the attack came.

The youngest was five; the oldest besides Lea was ten, and keeping them all alive in the wilderness had required a certain amount of military discipline. If Ari could get them to the foothills, Lea could lead them the rest of the way to Free Denver. The kids knew their chain of command.

Would Ari last that long? A series of wracking coughs seemed to answer in the negative.

Ari sat on the dirt-dusted stone floor, her arms wrapped tight around her spasming chest, fighting for an unhampered breath. She'd had pneumonia enough times to know it when she felt it.

There was nothing in her meager medical supplies that would combat this. She had no antibiotics left, and she'd used the last of her expectorants days earlier. The only thing left of any use was ibuprofen.

Ari fumbled the bottle out and opened it, shaking 1200 mg into her palm. She stared at the six pills, her heart aching. There were only two dozen tablets left. If she took six at a shot, she'd be out of them tomorrow.

What if Lea needs them? I'm wasting supplies. Ari slid four pills back into the bottle, closed it, and stashed it in the kit. She stared at her hand, rolling the other two between her thumb and palm.

I shouldn't take them. Lea might need them.

Ari had to make it as far as the foothills. She'd take as little as she could, until then. She dry-swallowed the 400 mg before she could argue herself out of it, tears pricking at her eyes.

A scream brought her head up.

Ari looked around, meeting Lea's startled expression and then finishing her head count. "Billy...and Noelle. Damn." Had she been so lost in thought that she hadn't realized they'd left the cave? Apparently so.

She pulled on David's ball cap, scrambling out the crevice with the useless .22 rifle in hand. Worst case, if her bluff failed, she could use it as a club.

Worst case, we'll all be dead. Or...

Now is the wrong time to entertain that thought.

They were everywhere, military types in camouflage. Ari would like to take heart in the differences between their markings and those of the traditional American armed forces, but truth be told, she'd been on the run so long, she didn't know which side had kept them...if either.

She picked out the two holding the struggling Billy and Noelle, noting how many she'd have to take down to give them a chance at escape. It was hopeless.

Only if they're on the wrong side.

Ari shifted the rifle, stroking the lock with a sweat-soaked finger. She damned David silently for not making sure she had a key to the lock in each of the sea bags. Whether she hated firearms or not, a functional weapon would go a long way toward ensuring their security.

He is so short-sighted. He'd promised Lea he'd meet them on the trail to Blue Top. He'd given his vow. As he had more than a few times in their lives together, David had let Lea and Ari down without hope of an apology for it.

Only this time, it might cost us our lives.

Wrong time to consider it!

She stared them down, waiting to see what would happen next.

The attack came without warning, a body hurtling at her. Ari turned toward him, bringing the rifle up to take his chin. It was too late; he hit her solidly, landing over her, his hand locking on the rifle over hers, crushing her fingers to the trigger lock and forcing the barrel to the side.

"Drop it," he ordered in a voice she'd dreamt of for more than a decade.

She met his eyes through her sunglasses. *Bain.* What was he doing here?

* * * *

Damn it! Why isn't he releasing the rifle? The leader wasn't fighting him, but he wasn't conceding defeat, either. What was his game?

In the next instant, a swarm of children appeared from inside the cave, pulling at Bain with curses and battle cries. Bain's men vaulted into the fray, dragging them away.

"Stand down," his prisoner ordered calmly. "Don't fight them."

Bain stared at her, shocked into a near-stupor. He examined the mud-pasted cap. The M.S.P. *It is... It has to be...*

He dragged the cap off, revealing black hair, cropped short and pasted to her head with sweat. "Ari."

A weak smile pulled up at her lips. "Hello, Bain."

He stared at her, taking in every detail in rising concern. She was trembling, and sweat coated her skin, though there was a decided chill in the air. Her breathing was rasping and uneven.

Bain cupped her cheek, cursing fluently at the heat radiating off of her. "Doc," he shouted.

Unbidden, the last time he'd seen her in this state coursed through his mind. He'd been guiding her back to bed, chiding her for walking around when she should be resting.

"What is it?" Matthews asked, appearing beside him. Matthews wasn't really a doctor, but he was the best they had on hand.

Ari started coughing, deep wracking coughs that had haunted more than a few of Bain's nightmares. He winced, hoping Doc had something appropriate on hand.

"Chief," Matthews prompted him.

"Yeah?" He didn't look around. It hardly seemed possible to look away from Ari now that he'd found her.

"You have to move, Chief. I need room to work."

Bain looked down at himself, acutely aware of his position, straddling Ari's thighs, leaning over her, one hand covering hers and the other planted on the ground next to her cheek. If he shifted, she'd know precisely how much her proximity affected him.

"Release the rifle, Ari." That was one chance he couldn't take, even for her. He had a duty to his men. *And my own skin.*

She laughed, a brittle sound, half-choking in the effort. He eased his grip on her trigger hand, allowing her to retreat.

The reason for her mirth became clear the moment her hand was clear and his closed around the rifle fully. There was a trigger lock in place. Ari couldn't have fired it, even if she'd wanted to. It had been a bluff.

Chapter Two

"How is she?"

Bain looked up from his place at Ari's side, depositing the rag back into the cool water with a plop. The girl was as tall as Ari, with the same long, black hair Ari had when he'd met her.

"Better. Her fever's coming down, but she's going to need some serious TLC when we get back."

He wasn't lying to her. He'd seen this before: antibiotics, steroids, cough suppressants, codeine, expectorants, fluids...

Matthews had done the best he could, considering the circumstances. He'd started an IV, injected a hefty amount of antibiotics and then a cocktail of painkillers and muscle relaxants Bain didn't even pretend to understand. The mixture had sent Ari into a decent sleep, during which her fever came down to a level he was more comfortable with.

"The sun's coming up," she noted.

Bain compared Lea to Ari. There was very little of David in her, at least outwardly. She seemed to have inherited a good deal of her father's attitude, if not his looks.

"Lea," he breathed. It had been David's idea to name her Lea. Ari had wanted to name her Jayde. He still didn't understand why Ari had knuckled under to him, but Ari had done that a lot in her marriage to David.

"Yeah?" she asked, her gaze locked on the cave entrance.

"Sorry. It's been a while." Eleven years and four months, to be precise. Lea had been just shy of two when Bain had seen her last.

She turned back to him, her brow creasing in confusion. "Since what?"

"Since I've seen you." He smiled at the memory. "You, running through the sprinklers in nothing but a Minnie Mouse swim diaper, as I recall."

Lea scowled at him. "So, you really knew my parents back then?"

Bain nodded. "Yeah. I knew them." That sobered him. He'd known them, all right. Would that their last meeting had been a better one. He focused on Ari, wondering yet again why she'd chosen as she had.

"You're Bainbridge Carter, aren't you? She called you Bain, so I figure you must be."

The fact that she knew his name shocked him, but he tried not to show it. "You've heard of me, huh?" But why had she and in what context?

Lea didn't answer that question. "What happens now?" she inquired coolly.

"We eat something and relax. When Ari's up to it, we head for the pick-up."

The growling of Lea's stomach brought his head up.

Bain scanned his gaze over the kids, huddled together along the opposite wall, whispering between themselves and shooting nervous glances at Bain and his men. He hadn't paid much attention to them until now. Lea had been handling them, and none of them had been a problem since Ari had ordered them to stand down.

But the reality of the situation had just slammed home. He had seven scared and hungry kids that needed tending to, and his men weren't going near them without orders to do it. Not after Lea's insistence that they keep their distance.

It was time to take command. "We'll get you something to eat."

They'd come prepared to feed a half dozen starving kids. Strangely, they looked fairly healthy, though not well fed. For that matter, they weren't nearly as dirty and ragged as he would have expected, given the nearly two months they'd been on the run after the sacking of the camp.

Lea took a step back, looking from Ari to Bain. "We have our own, thanks."

She marched between the dividing line of soldiers and sailors, scooping up one of two sorry-looking sea bags on the way. Lea dropped it in front of her young charges, and the kids gathered around her eagerly. Hands started reaching in, without delay.

"Remember," Lea instructed, "a handful of nuts and raisins...or a couple of the dried apricots we have left."

"Awww, Lea," a young girl of about seven complained.

"You can't live on crackers and nutrition bars, Noelle," she snapped. "It has to be fruit and protein, once a day."

"We have meat," Bain offered. It was freeze dried, jerky, and canned, but it was meat. Kids needed meat and milk.

The children stopped and stared.

Lea glared at him. "As I recall, *Chief*, my mother never said she trusted you. Until she does, we're not taking anything from you."

It was a challenge of his authority. It was a test, designed to see what Bain would do when challenged.

Lea waited for his answer. Several of the others shifted nervously, and a small, blonde girl ducked behind the cover of Lea's body, her hand leaving the sea bag entirely.

I'll have to choose my battles wisely. This was a little thing. "Go on then. I won't trample on Ari's authority. If she told you this was what she wanted you to do, then do it." But it was Ari's authority he was going to give credence to, not Lea's. Not outwardly.

Lea hesitated, a sure sign that Ari hadn't ordered this but none of them were about to admit it to him, then turned back to the other children. "Tell you what," she offered brightly. "This is a special occasion. Let's celebrate. One handful of the mix and one carb for everyone."

The kids dug into the sea bag, coming out with bags of Cheese Nips and Zwieback toast, nutrition bars, granola bars, and a baggie of something that resembled Fruit Loops.

"Milk?" the blonde asked.

Bain's move to answer was cut short by Lea.

"It's a celebration. I guess so. Billy, you earned E.M.I. Get the water."

"Awww, Lea–"

"Cut it."

The boy rose and headed for the entrance, scooping up a plastic bucket on the way.

Bain jerked his head to one side, ordering Cason along. All the children went still, the younger ones staring at Lea, Lea herself shooting silent question at Bain. He didn't comment. After a moment, she sighed and went back to her work feeding the kids. As if she'd given her consent, everyone started moving again.

Bain watched her efforts, his mind working hard at the problem of Ari's daughter. Lea was going to be a problem, he was sure.

As if David never was?

* * * *

"What the hell are you... You can't do that!"

Ari wrinkled her brow, coming half-awake. Her fuzzy mind seemed to take an inordinately long time to access the information about where she was and who owned the voice that woke her. *Bain's men.*

Lea's voice was laced with sarcasm. "What do you think comes out of your water faucet, numb nuts? Last time I checked, granted it's been a while, it's chlorinated water."

"You *cannot–*"

"Look! We couldn't get a portable UV pen. By the time my mom started collecting that high tech of gear, you know they had appropriated it all for the military, cut off civilian imports, and dedicated stateside manufacture for *official* purposes only. Even if we could get one, the purchase might have put us on a list to be among the first targets. So it's the old-fashioned way, bucko...unless you're offering a UV pen for us to use." She let the challenge hang between them.

"This isn't a good idea," he grumbled.

"Neither is taking in parasites or bacteria."

"Enough." That was Bain. "Lea... Do you know what you're doing?"

"No, Chief. I've been pouring blind for the last few months, and the Army survival manual I've all but memorized is wrong. That's why poor little me needs big, strong, highly-intelligent testosterone factories like you jerks to tell me how to–"

Ari started laughing, long and hard, setting off a vicious bout of coughing. In the next instant, she was being raised to sitting, a cup touching her lower lip. She pushed it away for a moment on the general principal that she didn't need to aspirate water; Ari had enough fluid in her lungs already.

When her lungs stopped protesting and her breathing eased a bit, she accepted the cup, nearly spitting in surprise that it was juice. The hand at her back rubbed in comfort that she didn't find comforting. Her heart drumming out a staccato response, Ari opened her eyes and focused on Bain.

He looked better than any man had a right to...and at a time when she looked like shit, no less. His blond hair was slightly longer than she remembered, but since he had a close clipper cut the last time she saw him, that only meant it brushed over his collar in the back. He had at least a two-day growth of beard, which she found intriguing and rather appealing on him.

No need to go there.

Ari went back to her examination of him. Bain hadn't changed much otherwise, though his green eyes were showing lines around the edges.

It was his eyes that held her longest. They were tired, yet so intense that Ari was torn between falling into them and looking away. The latter being impossible, more because of her need to believe she wasn't hallucinating his presence than their positions—though she'd lie under oath that it was just their positions locking her in his gaze—she indulged.

While we're indulging... Ari raised a hand and tracked a fingertip through his still-rough stubble.

"Ari?"

His voice rumbled out, sending a shiver down her spine. For a mad moment, she convinced herself that he'd shivered, as well.

Answer. Damn it, answer him. "I... You're real."

That curved his mouth into a smug little smile. "I'm real, and you're still not taking care of yourself."

Her breathing hitched at the same old words spilling from his lips. *Very kissable lips.*

Stop it! You screwed that up. Remember?

"Ari?"

"Mom," Lea's voice overlapped with his.

She forced her eyes away from Bain's and to her daughter's. "Can't help it," she managed. "I have too many other people to take care of."

His answer was crisp and uncompromising. "Learn."

Lea bristled. "Mom?"

"How's it going?" she asked, praying Lea would drop whatever she wanted to ask for a while.

Of course, that was a lost cause. Lea had too much of David's Mack truck subtlety to comply. "I don't know. Do we trust these guys or not?" She added a venomous look for Bain.

Ari shifted her gaze back to him, noting that Bain wasn't glaring back at Lea; he was staring at Ari. The shock of that gave way to a niggling of unease. She squelched the urge to squirm. Forcing her voice to emerge was hard, a fact she hoped she covered with a clearing of her suddenly dry throat.

"Which side are you on, Bain?" She kept it simple, straight-forward. They'd always been that way with each other. Well, she'd thought they had, until he'd dropped the bomb on her.

His face darkened a few notches, and his exasperation was impossible to miss. "We're Free Nationalists. You've been under a long–"

"I know which side is which." And he was the right side, by some stroke of dumb luck. Then again, Bain's ethics would indicate he'd take the Nationalist side.

She relaxed against him. "Thank God for huge favors," she breathed.

Lea launched right in. "Does that mean I can trust them?"

"Absolutely."

"Good, because they have meat, and peanuts are getting old. No offense. They were light, nutritious and all we had."

Ari sighed. "If they're offering food, take it. We still have a long walk to go." From the corner of her eye, she saw Matt nudge Liam toward the silent soldiers, and guilt ate at her. She'd had to ration them. Not knowing how long they'd have to depend on what little she had—

Bain's voice rumbled down at her. "How did you come to that one?"

She tipped her head back, searching out his inscrutable gaze. "If the way out was as simple as calling in air support, we'd be somewhere else by now."

"It's only ten miles away."

She nodded. "Then we can reach it tonight."

"Tonight? But you're–"

"Did I dream your corpsman saying he only had that single vial of penicillin? Did I dream him saying he was out?"

Bain paused, then shook his head.

"Then we have no choice. We've got a reprieve. Waiting isn't going to make me stronger. I'll start going downhill again very soon."

His jaw tightened, and he didn't answer.

"Besides that, we've had shadows for days. We can't stay here. If we do, they'll find us, and a firefight is the last thing you want. They'll lock down the entire area."

"Tonight then," he agreed. "Can you eat?"

Ari glanced at the pouches of food Lea was examining, her stomach rioting. "You know I can never eat like this."

"Unfortunately, I do."

* * * *

Bain called a halt, letting Ari's labored breathing lead the way, as he had been for the three hours it had taken them to make the first seven miles of their downhill trek to the rendezvous point. She half-sank, half-plopped to the mat of pine needles, trembling hard.

He crouched beside her, her sea bag, stuffed with his own gear and the last of hers, strapped to his back. "We can do the rest tomorrow," he offered.

She shook her head. "We're too exposed."

"But protected now," he reminded her. The irrational side of him wanted Ari to realize he'd protect her and for her to accept that protection.

"I just want to get out of here." Even in the semi-darkness, her haunted expression was hard to miss.

"Yeah. I'll bet." He pushed away the thought that "out of here" equated to "away from you."

Children, unsurprisingly wide-awake, and grumpy soldiers and sailors gathered around.

"Lea, get some food in their stomachs," Ari managed. "As soon as they've eaten, we'll start moving again."

Bain nodded his agreement, and his men broke out food and started distributing it.

"Are we going to Free Denver?" one boy piped up.

Ari's answer stopped Bain cold. "Maybe, Liam. The way the lines are drawn, we may not be able to fly directly into Free Denver. We'll get there as soon as we can, though."

"Yes," the boy cheered in a voice just above a whisper.

The tension from his men was impossible to miss. Bain cleared his throat. "Ari..."

She motioned him for silence, then waved Bain closer. He complied, his heart skipping at the first whisper against his ear.

"His father is supposed to be in Free Denver. Please, don't tell him that's where we're going. Not yet. Liam will think Joe will be there when we land if he knows."

Bain nodded, his mind spinning. "What do you know about his father? We'll have the flight in to find out what we can."

Her gasp of surprise heated his blood, and his mind locked on images of her gasping against his ear in bed, his cock buried to the hilt in her.

Bain forced it back. *This is the wrong time, the really wrong place. She doesn't even know about David yet.*

"His name is Joseph Wright. He's a Lieutenant...Navy. He was stationed at Coronado, before...before it hit the fan."

"Rating?"

"Not sure. He worked with the S.E.A.L.s. Parachute teams... In support, somewhere or other."

Bain nodded and settled to his heels again. "I'll see what I can do."

Ari opened her mouth to say something that never emerged. She shut it, a look he couldn't interpret on her face.

His examination was cut short by a sound he couldn't readily identify. It wasn't the wind or the scurrying of something small. Whatever this was, it was big...possibly human.

She opened her mouth to speak, and Bain covered it with his hand, motioning to his men with the other. He winced at her wide-eyed look and leaned to whisper in her ear again. "Shhh... Listen."

For a moment, the entire company was silent and still. Shy of Ari's breath against his fingers, there was nothing.

It came again, the rasp of something against dry leaves and pine needles. Bain motioned his men to get down and take cover. They, in turn, motioned to the kids and guided them to rocks and vegetation that would mask their presence. To Bain's shock, not a single child questioned the order. None of them whimpered, cried, or otherwise risked the group. They were as silent as his own men.

The sound moved closer, and Bain turned Ari to the ground beneath him, covering her with his body behind the screen of a leaf-bare bush.

"Are you sure?"

Ari shuddered at the sound of the voice. It couldn't have been more than twenty or thirty yards away.

"I heard something. I know I did."

"Are you—"

"Shut up, will you. If there is someone there, we might be able to hear them."

The woods went silent. Even the animals seemed to be hiding, waiting to see what would happen next.

Ari's back spasmed, most likely in a coughing fit she was trying desperately to force down. It was possible she'd lose that battle and give away their position.

Bain drew his side arm, sliding the safety off silently. He stretched his arm out past her head, shielded her ear, and settled the gun between the tangled stalks of the bush.

If worse came to worst, he'd have to take down as many as he could, before they could radio out...and pray there weren't more close enough to hear the shots. Failing all of that, Ari was right; the entire area would be locked down.

Ari shifted beneath him, and Bain closed his eyes, his cock coming up at the contact. He pressed his forehead to her hair, drinking in the smell of sweat and musk left after her midday scrub with the leftover water and camp soap, coupled with a change of clothing.

The sounds of men moving drew closer, and Ari's breathing went ragged against his hand. They ambled to within visual range, stopped to listen again, and Ari went tense.

All around them, there was silence. Bain didn't question that other weapons, like his own, were at the ready to take down the Federalists. He didn't question that the entire group, military and not, were saying prayers to whatever deities they believed in, even if that deity was Browning, Colt, or Smith and Wesson.

"There's nothing here," one groused. "You're hearing things."

A sigh answered. "Let's start back at that crossing. There was definitely someone there."

"Yeah. I don't know what they expect us to do out here. It's like looking for a rat in a haystack full of scurrying mice."

Their footsteps died away, and Bain relaxed against Ari's body, more comfortable than he should be, considering the circumstances. He didn't want to move, didn't want to abandon the close contact.

It was several minutes before Samuels' whispered assurances that they were well away brought people out of hiding. Bain eased off of Ari, aching at the loss of her heat.

She pushed to sitting, shaking hard. "Forget the food," she whispered. "Let's just move."

Bain nodded. "After that scare, I doubt anyone has an appetite left."

Chapter Three

August 31st

Ari stared out the window of the helo, her mouth dry. She glanced to Bain, noting his nod. *God, I hope this is right.*

Ellen had been so specific, but the scene from *Saving Private Ryan* kept looping in her mind. What if there were two Joe Wrights stationed in Free Denver? What if there was more than one with a son? How would they ever make this right for Joe and for Liam?

Of course, they hadn't told Liam that his father would be meeting them. Joe might understand; Liam wouldn't. At nine, he was too young to understand that they'd made that monumental a mistake. If the Joe Wright down there was the wrong one, they wouldn't say a word to Liam about it, and they'd search for his father in the coming days.

The rotors slowed, and the engines wound down. Two men in blue or black coveralls and safety orange vests jogged toward them, the pink-purple light of coming dawn at their backs, ball caps covering their bowed faces. One pulled the door open, and the other offered Ari his hand. She took it, stepping down onto free soil, her heart racing, though she couldn't tell if it was in joy or in the exhaustion wearing her down.

They'd made the three miles to the rendezvous site with barely a pause, Ari insisting they press on when Bain called halts. The Federalists had come too close to finding them, and she wasn't going to risk that again.

The kids could be silent, but they weren't adept at hiding their passing. If the enemy was tracking them, chances were they had a four-lane highway of clues to follow.

Bain followed her out, and the kids scrambled to their sides, Josie taking one of Ari's hands and Noelle the other. As a unit, they set out for the fifteen-man van waiting to transport them to medical.

There were a handful of soldiers and sailors milling around the vehicle. Ari took stock of them. One would be the driver of the van. Two had the distinct look of corpsmen or doctors. The last...

Ari looked at Liam and then back at the man in question, a smile pulling up at her lips. It was right. It had to be right.

The man took a step forward, his mouth opening in an 'o' of surprise. He recovered quickly, loping toward them, a smile breaking out on his face. "Liam," he shouted.

Liam's head came around, and he stopped short, his eyes widening. He shot a look of confusion at Ari.

"Go on," she counseled. "If he's your dad, don't leave him waiting."

Her breathing was ragged, rasping. For the first time in years, she couldn't wait to get to a hospital. Right now, a hospital meant a nebulizer, Prednisone, a hot shower, and a warm bed. Coughs wracked her, and her body felt leaden.

Liam didn't even pause long enough to nod. In the next moment, he was running full-out, throwing himself at his father. The sound of sobs and laughter reached her. Joe spun in place, holding his son to his chest as if afraid to ever let him out of his sight again.

The other men approached, the medical crew taking stock of their patients without laying a hand on them. "Remember, Lieutenant Wright," one cautioned. "Your son still has to be checked out. He might have to stay for a day or two, depending on what we find."

"I'm not leaving him," Joe stated firmly.

"We wouldn't suggest it."

He nodded, his eyes locking on Ari's. Shifting Liam to one arm, he offered his hand. She released Josie long enough to oblige him.

"I can't thank you enough," he choked out, tears making his eyes shine.

She nodded, at a loss to offer anything more. Her balance canted to one side, and Ari stumbled, crumpling into waiting hands. Lea's voice reached her through the buzz of overlapping sounds, and Bain's face swam in the fog of her vision. Then darkness dragged her down.

* * * *

Bain sat at her bedside, staring at Ari wearily. For the second time in as many days, she was drugged into a deep sleep. This time, she was scrubbed until her skin glowed an unnatural pink and tucked into a hospital bed, an IV in her arm.

Nurses and corpsmen had a heck of a time controlling the half dozen wired kids who wanted to be in the same room Ari was. Bain had finally convinced them to create a makeshift ward, where Lea could play stand-in buckaroo for the herd of young cats. On his last check on them, Lea and company were piled puppy-style onto two beds, humming a tune that Bain faintly recognized but couldn't place.

The only one missing from the collection was Liam, who was settled down in a room down the hall, his father crammed onto the narrow bed beside him. Joe had reported that Liam was so restless, he had to visit his traveling companions before he could sleep.

Now, Bain was back at Ari's bedside, exhausted, ripe from the days tracking her down and the rush to the hospital...and completely at a loss for what to do next.

"Chief?" Samuels called out. "Ready?"

Though it felt like an intrusion of privacy, he nodded and rose. It was time to catalog everything that Ari had in her possession when she was brought in. Since they had yet to find the microchips in anything left behind at Refugee Ridge, the wagers were that she literally hadn't let the object they were hidden in leave her sight.

Samuels and Jacobs had set up in the conference room at the end of the hall. Thanks to the Marine standing watch, neither of them had dared touch the sea bags and other supplies on the table.

His stomach churning, he reached for the first of them. "Let's get this over with."

Samuels took the other. Jacobs sat between them, recording everything they called out to him.

The lion's share of the nearly-empty bags was food. Even so, by his best estimate of the rationing she'd had them on, they had been down to less than a week's worth of food for the group.

Knowing Ari, she would have cut herself short before she cut the kids' rations. Then again, she didn't eat much when she was sick, and in her condition, that would have proven fatal for her in short order.

Ari's sweat-soaked outfit was shoved into the sea bag Bain had grabbed, and a spare outfit for Lea was folded in the other. The first aid kit was nearly depleted. Most of what was left would treat major injuries that they had thankfully managed to escape.

A grumbled curse from Samuels brought Bain's head up. The young soldier's brow was furrowed, and he was staring at something still tucked into the bag.

"What is it?" Bain asked.

Samuels' hand came out with a large box of dog biscuits. "One of these things is not like the other," he quipped.

Jacobs blanched. "You don't think..." He let the rest die off.

"That they had and resorted to eating a dog?" Bain finished for him. He shook his head, fighting back a smile at the sight of the box. "No. That had another use."

Samuels recovered enough to question that. "Mountain lions aren't dogs, Chief."

"No, and those aren't intended for mountain lions." He went back to the contents of the sea bag in front of him.

"Well what *is* it for?" Jacobs demanded.

Bain let a chuckle escape. "You really want to know this, don't you?"

"Yes." Their joint answer left no question that they wouldn't move on until they knew for sure.

He reached over and tapped a fingertip on the sealed top of the box. "Emergency rations."

Jacob made a rude sound and screwed his face up.

Samuels turned the box and considered the list of ingredients. "Not bad. I mean...gross, when you don't consider what's in these things, but they're probably the healthiest thing in this bag...besides the meal bars."

Bain refrained from telling them who'd taught Ari that trick. She used to keep a box around, just to watch him gross out the city kids. The fact that she was a city kid and found it hysterical had been one of the reasons he'd initially liked her.

"Chief?" Samuels called out, seemingly concerned.

"Sorry. Just a little beat. Let's finish this and get it over to the crew."

"One box of large dog biscuits," Jacobs called, his pen making neat block printing on the paper. He was still a little pale, but he didn't comment further.

The bottle of concentrated chlorine came out of Lea's bag next.

"I still don't understand why they didn't use the tried and true iodine trick," Samuels groused.

Bain sighed, turning a solar-powered LED flashlight in his hand. "Ari is allergic to iodine. It was a U.V. light pen or chlorine. They couldn't risk building fires or sun stills."

The room went silent.

Bain looked up at them, biting back a wince at their shock. "You guys knew I know her," he defended himself.

"How well?" Jacobs asked.

"Well enough and no better. Now, let's get this done. I need some rack time. Solar-powered LED flashlight. Plenty of places to hide the chips."

Jacobs hesitated long enough to earn a glare from Bain, then went back to his work.

A whistle from Samuels raised Bain's blood pressure.

"What now?" he snapped.

A velvet bag full of bits of gold made Bain's eyes widen.

"Hoolleee shit," Jacobs marveled. "That is one smart lady."

Bain reached over and stirred the snips of gold. "What the hell?"

Jacobs shook his head, his eyes wide. "Money. People that knew what was coming sometimes purchased gold chains and cut them into little pieces that could be easily traded. Bet there's a test kit in there for metals."

Samuels dug into the bag and came out with a clear plastic box that contained a variety of chemical bottles and a black stone rectangle. A rubber band around the outside held a wad of paper money to it.

"The bills are useless," Jacobs noted. "Good thing she didn't try to use them, on either side of the line. But..." He ran a fingertip through the gold. "Yeah, this would get her a couple thou on the black market, maybe half that, if she looked desperate enough to cheat."

Bain's jaw tightened at that pronouncement. "You seem to know a lot about the black market, Jacobs. Maybe more than you should know," he hinted.

The young quartermaster's face went a vivid red, and he seemed to be searching for words that wouldn't land him in the brig. "Sometimes we need supplies," he offered lamely. "Medical supplies. You know."

"Uh huh." Bain pulled a camouflage handkerchief out of his back pocket and dumped the gold into it. With one last swipe to make sure it was empty, he tossed the empty bag back to Samuels.

The other two men gaped at him.

"Besides David's insurance, this is all she has left in the world. There's no way the chips can be hidden inside the gold, right?"

Jacob's surveyed the pile of chain snips. "Not a chance."

"Then write it down with a note that I'll hold it for her until she's out of here."

Jacobs looked like he was about to argue.

"The black market gets the supplies they sell back to you by stealing them from our warehouses and trucks. Oldest game in town, Jacobs. Ari and Lea are not going to lose the last of what they have to some thief."

"I have to agree with the chief here," Samuels intoned.

Jacobs didn't answer. Instead, he wrote something on the sheet and handed it to Bain to sign. Content that it was what he'd ordered, Bain signed it and handed it to Samuels to co-sign. He tied the handkerchief up tight and tucked it into his pocket.

There were a few moments of uninterrupted work, broken only by Samuels and Bain calling out items to be cataloged and Jacobs echoing them as he wrote.

Samuels cleared his throat before announcing a box and a half of sanitary pads. That forced a chuckle from Bain, and he waved off their question of what he found funny about that.

Bain patted down the empty sea bag, then started checking the small pockets on the outside. One held waterproof matches, a Gerber knife, a compass, and flint. He pulled a camouflage handkerchief like his own out of the second.

His move to toss it on the growing pile short-circuited at the feeling of something hard shifting beneath his fingers. His heart hammering, Bain unfolded the handkerchief carefully. It wasn't the microchips inside. It was her rings, the engagement and wedding rings that tied her to David.

He stared at them. She'd likely taken them off to avoid someone seeing them...or to avoid damaging or losing them.

"Chief Carter?" Jacobs asked.

"One camo handkerchief." He paused. "One diamond engagement ring. One gold wedding band. Write down that I'm returning the rings to her." He reached for them.

"Whoa," Samuels called out. "That engagement ring could be it."

I hope so. Bain pushed that thought away. "Then she can turn it in herself."

"Chief–" Jacobs started.

"You don't take away a woman's rings."

"But he's–"

"She doesn't know that. For the moment, Ari doesn't *need* to know that. She needs to heal before she grieves." *And before she decides what to do with her life next.*

The other two stared at each other for a moment.

"You're probably right," Samuels conceded.

"I'll write it down," Jacobs added.

* * * *

Ari woke to something shaking the bed. Her eyes hadn't had a chance to focus when the bulk landed solidly on top of her, forcing the breath out of her bruised and abused lungs.

The rising panic sloped off at the little girl's arms circling her lower ribs. Instead, Ari indulged in a wry smile.

It was Josie. Besides her size, she was the only one that had latched onto Ari so markedly. Considering how young she was, that wasn't much of a surprise, but it was going to be difficult for both of them when they found her family. *If they find them.* Unlike the older kids, Josie knew very little about herself, save the name of her dead mother. Unless other relatives had listed them both in the database—and the search team could figure out how to spell the child's last name—she might just be unmatachable.

"Shouldn't you be with Lea?" Ari chided. The nurses were sure to be frantic when they couldn't find one of the kids. Lea, on the other hand, would know precisely where to look for Josie.

"Lea doesn't sing," Josie complained stubbornly.

Neither do I, right now. Not well, anyway. "It's going to sound weird, Josie," she warned.

"Don't care." The forty-odd pound kindergartener snuggled in and burrowed her feet under the blankets. A yawn followed.

Like I didn't know that would be the answer?

Ari sucked in a moderate breath and breathed out the strained words to "Let Joy and Innocence Prevail."

She'd been singing the song to Lea since birth, and it had just seemed natural to use it with the other kids, when she'd needed to build a routine into their shattered lives. Ari had to pause more often than usual, but Josie didn't seem to mind.

A squeak from the direction of the door convinced Ari to open her eyes. Bain stood in the doorway, listening to her. She faltered, then continued, knowing that Josie would be content with a single repetition but not with an aborted one.

There was something sad in Bain's eyes, something pained. As the song wound down, he moved toward the bed.

His hand came out silently, something held between his thumb and fingers. She raised hers to it, sure that he wanted to give her something.

The rings sent her heart skittering, and she stared at him, trying to understand what he meant by giving her rings to her? Was he simply returning them out of courtesy? Did he think she'd be frantic without them? Or was it something deeper? Maybe a reminder to both of them that there could be nothing between them, because she'd chosen David over him?

Forcing the words out to question him took more physical and emotional energy than she possessed. Instead, she nodded and closed her fist around the rings.

For the time being, she'd hang onto them. By the end of the week, she might be selling them. One thing that was certain was that she wouldn't feel guilty doing it.

Bain whispered out "good night" and was gone in the blink of an eye.

Chapter Four

September 3rd

"Coffee, ma'am?"

"She d–"

"Yes, please," Ari spoke over Bain. "Two creams. Two sugars."

"Yes, ma'am," the private replied smartly, preparing the coffee as requested and setting it in Ari's hand.

She nodded her thanks, then passed the mug to Lea, marveling at the way the military had become a mish-mash of the former services. Seeing Marines and Navy working together wasn't that uncommon, but the Army and Air Force in the same office as the Navy and Marines was rather disconcerting for her.

Her daughter took a drink and then hummed in pleasure. "Oh, yeah. I missed that."

"Then you won't mind running herd for a while," Ari suggested, jerking her head toward the hallway. She feigned amusement, trying desperately to hide her true feelings.

She had to get Lea out of this meeting. Chances were, there were things that would be said, things that Lea shouldn't hear in the blunt manner they were likely to be delivered.

Lea scowled but she rose and shuffled off, shutting the door behind her.

Ari settled back in her chair, her smile fading at the sight of Bain. He stared at her, seemingly caught between frustration and confusion.

"No, Bain," she assured him. "I've never liked coffee, and I never will. Lea picked that bad habit up from David." One of many, but luckily Ari had gotten used to them with her husband.

A smile pulled up at his lips. "Private, do we have orange juice hanging around somewhere?"

"Right away." He hurried to the small fridge in the corner of Elias's office.

"Aye, aye, sir," she joked in return. "Sorry...Chief. You work for a living."

Bain cleared his throat, shifting his gaze toward the officer behind the desk. Ari turned to him, keeping her expression neutral. Either Captain Elias had resigned himself to that joke long ago, or he was the sort of pompous, useless type that the joke poked fun at anyway.

Captain Elias sighed, shooting a weary look at Bain. "I see why you like her, Carter."

Ari skirted a peek at Bain's blush, then away. There had been a time that they'd liked each other very much, but that had been long ago.

It would be a good idea to change the subject, before they got into very uncomfortable areas. "You need something." Cutting to the chase was probably her strongest move.

Elias nodded. "Very astute."

"You're fighting a war. Rescue missions... I'll buy that, but then you'd turn them over to civilians for all but a debriefing."

"You're right," he conceded. "That is what we typically do."

"But...not with us." They'd spent three days at the military hospital, treated better than she'd ever been treated at Charette Naval, and had only undergone the most basic debriefing. Now they were at Free Denver WesCom, and they were there for a reason.

There was a moment of tense silence that made the hair on the back of her neck stand on end.

Elias's gaze bored into her. "Do you know what we're looking for?"

Ari considered that. "Not a clue." What did she know? She'd been in the backwater of a war zone for more than four months, avoiding contacts that could make her an inadvertent scout for either side.

Elias shot a look practically begging aid at Bain. "I was afraid of this," the Captain muttered.

Ari turned to the younger man. For some reason, Bain looked discomfited.

"Before..." He paused, wincing at something she couldn't name. "David said that–"

Her heart stuttered. "David? He's here?" When he didn't join them along the refugee trail, she'd assumed he'd blundered into Blue Top as she'd almost done, that he'd been killed there.

"No." Bain took a deep breath and straightened, meeting her eyes. "He's gone, Ari. More than two and a half months ago."

She nodded, attempting to swallow the sour lump building in her throat. Then she had to tell Lea her father was dead, after all. Not that it would be a shock. By the time they'd settled into the mountains, Lea had come to grips with the fact that her father must be dead, if he hadn't come for her.

* * * *

Bain watched the color drain from her face. Ari pressed the fingers of one hand to her mouth, swallowing hard.

The private returned and tried to offer her the orange juice, but she pushed it away. Bain took it, set it on the edge of the desk, and waved him toward the hall. The door closed behind him.

Finding words was even harder after he'd broken the news. "Ari–"

"No." She exhaled, more breathing the word than speaking it. "I've known for a long time...suspected, I guess."

Bain nodded, his jaw tightening reflexively. *Of course. Because, David would have come for her, if he could. She's never gotten over that damned knight in shining armor, starry-eyed view of him.* This had to be shattering for her. He fisted his hands, a silent reminder not to try to physically comfort her in front of Elias.

"How?" she asked.

"What?" He'd lost track of the conversation.

"How did David die? I have to tell Lea something."

He couldn't keep his mouth shut, as usual. He threw his life away with one too many smartass comments to the wrong person. That was David... Winning friends and influencing people all over the place.

Come on, Bain! Think a little. She's not going to tell her kid that. You don't want her to.

123

"Bain?"

He met her eyes again, wondering at when he'd allowed his gaze to drift away. "Gut shot by a Federalist soldier. Too far from a hospital. It was over quickly." It was all true and yet not the whole story. David had been dead before they'd cleared the city limits.

She nodded solemnly. "Right. Well, if he said something, he wasn't alone. David always said he'd die alone."

Bain's jaw clenched in the memory of David's last coherent moments. It might have been better, if he'd been alone. It was typical David, of course. He wanted Bain's promise to do him a favor, and still his animosity at the fact that Bain would carry through had lent a rough edge to every word David had spoken.

Ari's sharp intake of breath brought his gaze up again. She stared at him, her eyes pleading. Her mouth opened, shut, and she swallowed hard. "You?" That single word managed to convey a wealth of conflicting emotion.

"Yeah. I tried to get him out, but I got there a little too late."

"Did he...leave any message for me?"

"Just to take care of Lea for him." It was the honest answer, though he'd rather lie to her.

No. I've never lied to her. I may have hidden what I felt for her, but I never lied to her.

A glance at her tight-lipped grin and the shake of her head confirmed that he'd made the right choice. It had been eleven years. Any lie he told her would have been a minefield. It apparently wasn't a surprise that David hadn't left words of love and loss for her.

"So, what did he say?" Ari asked.

Bain stared at her, trying desperately to follow her jumps of topic, though he'd always managed that well enough before.

"What did David tell you I had for you?"

"Microchips."

Her brow furrowed in confusion, and she shook her head in a negative response.

"David said they were hidden in something he gave you."

"Well, that does sound like something David would do," she groused.

"Something he told you never to part with, never to let out of your sight," he qualified. Maybe that would spark a memory for her.

"And that doesn't."

"There has to be something, Ari. Think about it for a few days." Bain tried not to plead. "Maybe you just forgot that he–"

Her eyes narrowed in anger. Ari pulled off the wedding band and engagement ring she still wore and slammed them onto the edge of Elias's desk so hard the old man jumped.

"This was the only thing David was ever anal about me not losing. Tear them apart...carefully. Remember how small microchips can be these days. I wouldn't want you to destroy what you need."

Elias cleared his throat. "You'll get them back when we're–"

"Don't bother," she snapped. "Why would I need them?" But her eyes said that hurt when her words announced that it didn't.

Elias looked to Bain, turning the highly volatile situation over to the man who knew her, but even Bain wasn't certain how to handle this one. Maybe a change of topic would be best.

"We've found Billy's grandparents," he told her. "They're all the way in San Diego, but we can have them here to pick him up within a matter of days. A week, at the most. Matt's older brother Mike is stationed at the front. Given the circumstances, he's being transferred back here to take custody of Matt."

"That's good."

"He's done his time, and this lists him as the single parent to Matt. I can't imagine he'll be sent back." Bain was sure she'd worry about that. "We may have a lead on an aunt for Noelle. Since both of her parents are dead, like Matt's... We expedited the searches, but we won't call in family until we've established that they're the right family."

They'd found Stephanie's mother within hours. Even with the database, that had been impressive work.

Ari nodded. "I'll let them know."

"Is there anything more you can tell us about Josie?" The little blonde heartbreaker seemed the only one that was going to be impossible to trace someone for.

She sighed, worn by the pneumonia and the stress of the day, no doubt. "They'd just shown up a day before. I'm not even sure how to spell their last name, and Josie is no help with that." She rubbed the pads of the index and middle fingers of both hands into her temples. "It was all her mother could do to let Josie out of her sight long enough to play with the other kids while she talked to the camp council."

"Yeah. Good thing she did." If she'd decided to keep Josie with her, the child would be dead, like everyone else that had been slaughtered that day...women, children, the elderly.

Ari didn't reply immediately. "Yeah. Life and death are just a comedy of errors."

Bain didn't have an answer for that. "Come on. I'll take you home."

Her eyes questioned him.

"It's a house big enough. Base housing, but big enough. We've got bunk beds in the kids' rooms. We've stocked it with food and a few outfits each."

Still she stared, her expression unreadable.

"We'll get more in a few days," he soothed her. "I didn't want to pick too much for you."

"No. It's not that."

He waited patiently for the explanation.

"It's been almost two months since I've had more than two outfits to my name. And, aside from the hospital beds, I haven't slept in a bed in so long that I've forgotten what a real one feels like."

Bain managed a tense smile, his mind treading down paths it shouldn't. Like what sharing a bed with her would be like.

There was little chance of that. Who knew what she'd think of the living arrangements, as it was.

* * * *

The house wasn't huge, but it was bigger than any military housing she'd ever seen, and it was also better built. When she commented on that, Bain imparted that the military had commandeered several large neighborhoods that had been abandoned when the fighting got too close. Most of the personal belongings left behind had been moved into storage units, in case the owners eventually returned.

The fences to create the military bases had gone up nearly overnight, and the Free Denver WesCom had been born.

The house was a four-bedroom unit. Bain had arranged for beds to accommodate the kids remaining. Excess beds would be sent back to supply when they weren't needed.

Josie and Noelle were sharing a set of bunk beds in the furthest room to the right of the stairs. Lea had a full-sized bed in the same room. Ari's room came complete with a queen-sized bed. Between the girls' room and hers, there was a full bath.

To the left of the stairs, was Bain's room, a master bedroom with an attached bath. That way, he'd explained, there would be no accidents with Bain walking in on the girls.

Beyond his room was the smallest of the bedrooms. It had been outfitted with bunk beds for Billy and Matt. Bain had left it to Ari to decide if the boys would share the master bath with him or share the hall bath with the girls and Ari. He'd opined that there was no reason they couldn't share his.

"Ari?" he prodded, bringing her back to the here and now. "Should the boys use my bathroom or the one you and the girls are using?"

She hesitated, unsure of how to answer him. Ari wasn't certain what to make of the fact that Bain would be living with them. She tried to convince herself that he'd been assigned to them until the elusive microchips were located.

"Here." He reached for the doorknob to his room. "I'll show you the bathroom and let you decide."

Something in his expression rattled her. She didn't want him to open that door. There was something too personal in the move...too private. Ari didn't even know if his belongings were in there yet, but she was spooked at the idea of the intimacy of seeing them.

"No." She placed her hand over his, indicating that he shouldn't open the room.

Bain looked up at her, questioning the move.

Ari pulled her hand back, trying to make sense of the confusion touching him caused. "No. The boys can make up their minds. If they're comfortable with sharing your bathroom...sure."

That accomplished, she hurried to the stairs and down, trying to pretend she hadn't seen Lea's questioning look.

He followed her. "Ari?"

"Just want to see the rest of the house," she lied. At the bottom of the stairs, she stopped to catch her breath, her head spinning at the exertion.

His hand closed on her shoulder, and Bain surveyed her face. "Are you okay?"

"Yeah. Just a little lightheaded."

He led her away from the stairs but not toward the living room. To her surprise, Bain led her through the kitchen and the open door to the laundry room. Beyond them was a small den. Her mouth went dry at the sight of the futon.

Bain was all business. He helped her down onto the surface and told her to relax while he got her a glass of water. Then he was gone.

All business. I thought he was all business back then, too. Or, at least, just playing the part of a concerned friend.

That forced a groan up her throat.

* * * *

"Feeling better?" Bain asked.

Ari certainly looked better than she had at the base of the stairs. Hell, she looked better than she had upstairs.

Even now, he wasn't sure what had spooked her. Bain wished to hell he did know. Months on the run or not, something had happened in that hallway that went beyond those traumas.

"Much. Thanks for the water...and the help." She didn't look up at him. It seemed Ari wanted to pretend that she found something very interesting in the water glass.

"Do you feel up to helping me with something?" He had to tread lightly and try not to spook her.

That brought her gaze up to his face. "As long as it doesn't involve heavy lifting," she joked.

"Ha ha ha. No." Bain slipped the list from his pocket and set it on the table in front of him. "We've done a preliminary search on everything, of course. It would speed up the full search, if we could focus only on things David gave you."

Points of color flared in her cheeks. "Sure. how do you want me to mark them?"

He handed her a pen. "Just cross off anything he didn't give you. We'll go down the list of things he did first and then go back to anything leftover, if we haven't found the chips at that point."

The list was extensive, everything she'd had when they found her—on her body and in both sea bags—and everything that had been in her van.

Ari moved slowly, considering each item carefully. At times, she started to cross one off and then left it. It was Bain's guess that she was uncertain whether David had purchased it or not. Or maybe she was evaluating whether David would perceive that he had given it to her. That was a very real possibility, with David in the picture.

The van came last. She deliberated for longer than most of the others.

"Problem?" he asked.

"No. David picked the model and bought it, so I guess he gave me that. He never told me not to let it out of my sight, though. He never said that about any of this stuff." There was a note of disappointment in her voice.

Bain nodded. "That's okay. At least we have somewhere to start. They have to be somewhere."

"What if they're not, Bain?"

That set off alarm bells. "You have reason to believe they won't be?"

Ari shrugged. "I don't remember him ever telling me not to let something out of my sight. What if it's something that got left behind? What if it's something I traded? I mean... I only remember trading food, but what if I'm wrong?"

Then we're screwed. "I don't know. If that happened, we'll just have to do some research to recreate the chips." But that would take a year, at best, probably longer.

* * * *

September 9ᵗʰ

Lea carried the baking dish to the table, setting it on the trivet Ari had set out for it.

Bain inhaled the glorious scent, then winced. It was tuna casserole. Ari had surely forgotten that he couldn't eat mushrooms, and he'd be heading for a sandwich shortly. The trick would be doing that without making her feel guilty for forgetting.

"What's wrong, Chief?" Lea asked. "Don't like tuna or something?"

Like her dad. David had hated anything heated that included tuna. No tuna melts. No tuna casserole. No macaroni and cheese with tuna. For years, Bain had thought of Ari when he'd had one of those meals. It was something she only made when David had duty, because her husband wouldn't eat it. He hadn't even liked the smell of it cooking.

Ari laughed and answered before he could. "No. He's allergic to mushrooms." Her eyes glittered in amusement. "Which was why I made it with cream of celery soup, just like I used to for you, so eat up, sailor."

His shock that she remembered set loose a swarm of butterflies in his stomach. "You did that for me? How the hell did you remember it?" It wasn't as if she'd made him tuna casserole often. Only a handful of times over three years. But she'd remembered that little detail.

She started scooping the casserole onto plates for the kids, a secretive little smile on her face. "That's not all I remember. You're also allergic to blue cheese dressing, and you absolutely hate grapefruit juice." Her nose wrinkled.

"And so do you," he recalled. "And pepperoni...and kiwi." Bain knew why he remembered her likes and dislikes. Obsession does that to a person. But why did she remember his?

As if answering his earlier question, Lea shot him a dirty look. "If you know her so well, why don't you know she has the memory of an elephant? The woman never forgets anything."

Ari laughed at the comment, shaking her head.

She didn't see the dirty look. What would her reaction have been to that?

Bain wasn't about to tattle on Lea just to find out. He wasn't going to demand an answer from the teen, either. Eventually, they would have to make peace, but it seemed Lea wasn't ready for that yet. Bain wasn't sure he was ready to stand up to whatever Ari's daughter had to say to him.

David's daughter. Whatever is wrong with her, it's likely something to do with her father more than her mother. The kid had just found out she'd lost her father. From her point of view, even showing interest in her mother was inappropriate.

It is inappropriate. But Ari seemed strangely unaffected by David's death.

She said she'd known in her heart for a while. Maybe she'd already done her grieving, but Lea hadn't. He had to keep that in mind.

At last, Ari looked up. Her smile faded, and she darkened in a blush, sending him more mixed signals that drove him crazy to know what was on her mind. Ari reached her hand out, hinting for his plate.

He handed it over, forcing a smile for her. "I missed your cooking," he admitted.

"After being on the run for so long, let's hope I remember how to cook real food."

Josie spoke through a mouthful of casserole with all the decorum of most children her age. "You do."

That was all it took to get Ari laughing again.

Chapter Five

September 11th

Ari poured the leftovers into a large bowl, more than aware of Bain standing an arm's-length behind her. She took her time, avoiding his eyes.

It made no sense to be so nervous. They were friends.

Yeah, right.

Well, they had been friends...before. At one point, they could have been much more than friends, but it hadn't worked out that way. It was ancient history.

And so is our friendship.

"I think the pot's empty, Ari."

She glanced down, realizing she was idly scraping at metal. She set it back on the cold burner, sealed the bowl and headed to the fridge.

His footsteps sent her heart skittering. Part of her urged Ari to look back at him. Another part didn't want to be trapped in the hell of watching his expressions and guessing at what they meant.

Ari had been playing that game for almost two weeks. One minute, they slipped back into the same old jokes, turning the clock back. The next, his expression was intense, his eyes pleading, or his words cryptic. Not knowing what he wanted was driving her insane. Painting everything with her own hopes left Ari confused about what she was seeing and what she was imagining.

She stored the bowl in the fridge, mentally calculating that it would be gone by dinner the next day, and shut the door. Her mind in a riot, Ari fished for anything she could do that didn't involve turning back toward Bain and his unfathomable expressions.

"Are we ever going to work this out?" he asked.

"I thought we had, more than eleven years ago," she managed calmly. "You said we couldn't go back. I said we couldn't go forward. You said there was nothing left to talk about. You made that more than clear when you walked away."

Ari cursed herself for saying the last part. She'd sent him away. She'd given Bain no choice in the matter. The shards left of their friendship were her own fault.

Bain grasped her by the shoulder and turned Ari toward him. For a moment, he loomed over her, his jaw notched down tight and his eyes hard. Ari sank back to the refrigerator door, her knees trembling.

It wasn't that she was afraid he'd hurt her. That was one thing she'd never had to fear with Bain. If anything, she was afraid of her own reactions, of what she wanted to happen next.

Bain's voice was calm, resonating confidence in his decision. "I'm done talking."

With that, he brought his mouth down on hers. Ari's eyes slid shut, and her heart pounded for a new reason.

For all that he was staking a claim, it was done gently...a slow stroll of his lips against hers. His hand left her shoulder and trailed down her arm and then her ribs, curling around her hip.

She kissed at his lower lip, then the upper, tilting her head in encouragement. Their lips separated but not by much. Bain's breath warmed her, and their panting breaths accomplished delicious little touches of their now-sensitized mouths. Bain moved his head in a nodding motion, flicking at her lips with his own, growing more purposeful as she followed suit.

The change from teasing touches to a full-blown carnal exploration came so fast it made Ari dizzy. One moment, they were engaging in hard little pecks. The next, their lips parted, and tongues curled past and into uncharted territory.

In the moment after that—or at least the next that made sense—they were crushed together against the fridge door, Bain's fingers splayed across her lower back, beneath her sweatshirt, their mouths meshed tight.

"Ahhh-ri," Josie called out from somewhere beyond the kitchen door.

Bain broke away from her, his expression as unreadable as it had been all night. Ari took a moment to catch her breath, her body and mind in a riot. He stroked his fingertip down her lips silently and moved a body length away.

She started to turn, stopping to stare at the bulge in the front of his jeans, her mouth going dry. Bain took her hand and drew it to him, pressing it flush to his cock beneath his hand, smiling at her shiver of delight.

"Ah-ri."

He released her, his eyes hot in promise. "After bedtime, we're going forward," he whispered.

Ari's body reacted fiercely to that.

"Answer her."

She realized she still had her hand pressed to his crotch and slid it away, abruptly self-conscious. "Yes, Josie?" she yelled back.

Bain circled her, standing behind her, a portion of his body hidden by hers. Ari tried not to consider how much was. Would anyone see his erection, as they stood?

As if in answer, Bain pressed his hips forward, his cock settling far out on her left butt cheek. He straightened as the door burst open.

Josie hurtled in, coming to a stop halfway between the door and their positions, her little face screwed up in anger. "Lea says I have ta go to bed," she complained.

"You all do," Ari replied patiently. "You start school tomorrow. That means a good night's rest."

"Now you sound like a mother. I thought we were a unit."

Ari chuckled. "Even units have military discipline, and right now, the standing order is bed."

Josie's move to protest was cut short by Bain's gruff voice of command.

"Is there a problem here?" he asked. "Does this situation call for E.M.I.?"

Josie looked up at him in surprise.

Ari decided to play along. "No, Chief. I believe our young sailor is on her way."

He grunted his agreement. "Carry on, then."

Josie's eyes widened, and she bolted for the stairs. Ari chuckled at her reaction to the mention of extra military instruction...extra chores.

The chuckle choked off at the sensation of Bain's hand, starting at her hip and sliding down the front of her jeans to the already-damp cleft between her thighs. His voice rustled the hair around her right ear.

"I'm hungry. Don't take long."

As much as she ached to be his dessert, the kids weren't going to fall asleep the minute their heads hit the pillows. "Bain, we–"

"The den," he qualified, circling his fingers over her clit.

The den was downstairs, at the far end of the house. Better, there was a lock on the door and a futon.

She nodded, already dreading the delay.

* * * *

Bain started to pace, then forced his feet to the floor. He wiped his sweating palms on his jeans, cursing his nerves.

He'd been dreaming of this day for the last twelve years.

Longer. Oh, yes. It had been longer. Truth be told, Bain had wanted Ari since the day he met her. "Fifteen years," he breathed.

They'd been young, impossibly so, it seemed. Ari had been eighteen and Bain and David only twenty.

She'd already been David's, of course, his girl from back home. An unreasoning jealousy had gripped Bain at that. Why couldn't Ari have grown up in the Midwest, where she could have made out with Bain under the stars, instead of in New England, where she'd petted with David in parked cars?

David had been Bain's best friend, and so Bain had pretended nothing was wrong. He'd become Ari's 'friend,' spending as much time laughing and talking with her as he could.

He'd stood as David's best man at their wedding.

Bain snorted at the irony in that. He'd always felt he was the better man for her, the best man in a more concrete manner.

But she'd seemed happy with David, so he'd kept his mouth shut and stood at the altar beside the man he envied, envisioning himself on the honeymoon with Ari, instead of that child in a grown-up's body.

Using the loosest definitions of the terms, Bain had cornered the market on at least five of the deadly sins that day. If he could have fit in gluttony and sloth, he would have had a matched set. As it was, alcohol had been the only thing Bain could stomach that day...and for several days afterward, and the last thing he wanted to do was nothing.

And yet he'd done nothing...at least as far as making his wants known to her.

David had hardly qualified as husband of the year. He'd been a little closer to father of the year. Still, things weren't as rosy as they'd seemed those first few years.

The cracks appearing in their marriage had cracked Bain. He still couldn't believe he'd picked that moment to fumble into the concept that there were other men...other men that wanted her, that she didn't have to stay where she seemed to be so miserable. In retrospect, he'd sounded like a cross between a stalker and an insensitive jerk, he was certain.

And then he'd kissed her. It had been an invitation, more enticement than demand, and for a single, heart-stopping second, it had seemed she'd been enticed. Then she'd pushed away, her regret and embarrassment all too clear, stammering out an excuse to run from him.

Far short of convincing Ari she should leave David, it had cemented her resolve to make it work with him. The next time he'd seen her had been the last. The words *I can't do this, Bain. I won't do it.* were seared in his memory. She'd wanted things to be the same, but that was something Bain hadn't been able to do.

He couldn't stand by and watch her hurting, knowing he was the best man for her, waiting for a day that might never come. Ari had made a choice, knowing there was an option.

Bain had gone his own way, but he'd left her a way to reach him. For a year or two, he'd hoped she'd use it, but she never had. After that, he'd written off the encounter as a lost cause.

"Finders keepers," he whispered. David could cry in his grave, for all Bain cared. He'd thrown Ari away when he'd gotten himself killed. It had been an idiot move, but stupidity should be painful. For David, it had been.

Bain pulled off his sweatshirt and tossed it over the back of the recliner. Whether they made it past kissing and touching tonight or not—and Bain wasn't going to push for it—he wanted to feel Ari's hair on his skin.

As if the thought conjured her, the lady in question slipped through the door and locked it behind her. She looked up at Bain, her eyes going wide and her gaze panning over him.

He strode to her, cupping Ari's cheeks in his hands and drawing her face up. Her eyes slipped shut, and she met him with parted lips.

As in the kitchen, they came together hard and fast. Bain ran his hands through Ari's hair, then down her back, delving beneath the back of her sweatshirt, shivering at the skin-to-skin contact. He guided her further into the room, to the futon. Ari didn't shy from the idea; she pressed to him, her hands stroking at his bare chest.

Bain lifted her slightly, turning her with him as he dropped to his knees on the futon. Ari stretched out on the down-filled blanket he'd dragged downstairs from his bed, her eyes opening. His heart pounded at the invitation...the longing, he hoped.

He followed her down, enjoying the press of his body to hers, the fit of her curves to the planes of his. Ari panted out something incoherent. Bain lowered his head, weaving his face slowly, side to side, heating her lips with his breath, seeking hers in return.

"Bain," she pleaded.

Hell, yes.

In the moment following, their mouths were meshed together. The next truly coherent thought he had was that her sweatshirt was inching up, bringing them belly-to-belly. Bain pushed up on his hands, giving her room to remove it.

Ari didn't hesitate; she dragged the fleece up, uncovering a red satin bra that made Bain's mouth water. If he'd known she'd bought things like this with her stipend, he would have been hard every minute he spent in the same room with her.

She leaned up, working the fabric over her shoulders. Bain took advantage of the position, unhooking the bra one-handed...and she froze.

There was no plea for him to stop. Ari didn't seem to breathe.

Bain considered his options, quickly weeding them down to the one that felt right. She wasn't asking him to stop, and until she did, he was going to explore. Bain drew his hand to the front, his thumb over the satin and his fingers beneath. He cupped her breast in his fingers, stroking the satin back and forth over her hardening nipple.

Ari pulled the sweatshirt over her head and dropped it behind her. Her dark eyes opened, and she stared up at him, little gasps punctuating her rapid breathing.

He released the satin completely, sliding his thumb beneath to stimulate her reaction directly, smiling as it came to a harder point against the pad of his thumb. Ari eased the bra down her arms, uncovering herself. Bain took advantage of it, sliding toward the foot of the futon and lowering his face to suck at the other.

She bowed up, one hand tunneling through his hair, her breathing harsh but not in a way that worried him. No, this sound was one that had him weeping precum and coming to a near-painful erection against her thigh.

The drive to push her higher was maddening. Bain moved from one breast to the other, pushing up at her back to force her further into his mouth.

* * * *

This is crazy.

As if in answer, Bain's sucking became more insistent. His cock pressed to her inner thigh through the layers of their jeans, wringing a gasp from her that seemed to egg him on.

They were like two kids petting in a parked car. It was more than arousing. It held an edge of the forbidden, a delicious bite of anticipation and risk.

On that thought, Ari cupped her hand over his cock, squeezing gently. Bain's face came up, her nipple sliding free of his mouth. His eyes opened, and he waited for her next move.

Her heart pounding, Ari started stroking him. Bain moaned, watching her, his gaze hot and hungry. His fingers trailed up the inside seam of her jeans, pausing at the soaked cleft for a moment, then circling her clit.

Ari's cry of delight was smothered in his ravenous kiss, his body settling over hers again, their tongues engaged in a wild dance that matched her heart rhythm. Bain moved her hand, pressing it to the blanket as he started thrusting against her. A mutual moan mingled in their mouths.

Oh , God. I forgot how good a dry hump can feel.

Then again, there was nothing dry about this. She was wet and ready, and the residual moisture from the front of his jeans said he was, too.

She could come this way, all too easily, but she ached for more, throbbed in a drumbeat of anticipation. Her want to consummate with him as she should have more than a decade earlier was fast becoming a need.

Ari worked her free hand between their bodies, pulling at the button on Bain's jeans. He went still, the kiss shallowing but not ending. She slid the zipper down, and Bain plundered her mouth again. He left the kiss completely at the first touch of her fingers on the silken shaft, whispering his encouragement.

She massaged the sweet spot just beneath the head, smiling at his panting breaths. "Free-balling," she teased, circling the now-wet head with her thumb. "I like it."

"For you," he admitted. "I wanted as little as possible between us."

"Then get less between us." It was an offer and a plea, rolled into one.

Bain rolled to his side, drawing Ari along with him. He nestled his face to hers, nipping at her lips while he undid her jeans.

She pushed his away, baring Bain to the thighs, playing at his sac and then his weeping cock. Her move to taste him was brought to a halt by his next move.

It was a quick, decisive yank that took her jeans to her knees. In the next instant, his hand was inside her panties, two fingers thrusting inside her, stretching her deliciously, the heel of his hand grinding at her clit. Ari's cry escaped into the room, and Bain started pumping his fingers harder.

His words teased at her sensitized lips. "Say I can, Ari."

She didn't question what he meant. "Yes. Oh, yes."

His hand was abruptly gone, and her panties and jeans left her body in a stinging rush. A heartbeat or two later, she was on her back, Bain's larger body covering hers, his thighs forcing hers apart, his cock sliding home.

His shout overpowered hers, both echoing on the stark brick of the fireplace. Ari wrapped her legs around his hips, moaning as Bain withdrew halfway then thrust deeper.

"Oh, yes," she repeated. "Please, Bain. Don't stop."

He didn't. If the kiss in the kitchen was staking a claim, his sex was branding her as his. It was beyond hot, scorching pleasure and need through her. Their mouths met and parted, their bodies sliding against each other, slick in sweat and musk.

Her orgasm ramped up at the nip at her earlobe and the rumble of his voice against her hair.

"This is only the beginning, Ari." His pause and moan set her heart stuttering. "Say I can, and this is nothing compared to what's in store."

All the time, his pistoning hips were driving her over the edge. Ari teetered on the precipice already, one hand grasping at his shoulder and the other fisted in his hair, her body rising in time to his.

"Say I can, Ari." It wasn't an order...or a plea. It was a dark seduction.

"You can," she managed. Oh, but she wanted him to.

His thrusts speeded, and a harsh curse left his lips. "Come for me."

As if I have a choice? Ari didn't want a choice.

His cock bucked inside her, releasing a hint of warmth. At her limits, Ari arched against him, the contractions so hard they stole her breath.

Bain cried out softly, freezing deep inside her, wave after wave of his cum buffeting her. Climax had reduced her to a mass of raw nerves, and the force of his release sizzled at every one of them, pops and crackles of sensation making her entire body weak and receptive.

It was wild, draining, better than Ari could remember ever feeling before. She opened her eyes, meeting the green of Bain's.

At the connection, his cock twitched, then hardened more forcefully. Ari pushed her hips up, shock and arousal fueling her hunger.

The second time was slower, and Ari took the superior, taking him to the root at nearly every meeting of their bodies. Hands and mouths sampled, and the rise to climax was gentle. In the aftermath, she lay over him, deliciously sated, their mouths meshed as his cock softened within her. She was certain Bain hadn't come a second time, but he hadn't gone flaccid while he got her off again.

Finally, his length slid free of her. Ari broke the kiss on a sigh, burying her face in his throat. His scent surrounded her, comforting yet not.

His hand stroked up and down the line of her spine, and his lips nestled to her hair. Neither of them spoke.

Ari bit at her lower lip, abruptly nervous. The silence seemed to press down on her, and her heart pounded in apprehension.

Bain's hand cupped her cheek, and his lips pressed to her forehead. "Hey, I'm here," he whispered. "I'm here."

She nodded, her breathing choppy. Yes, he was here, and so was she, but Ari couldn't justify her actions.

A week after learning my husband is dead? What am I doing? Am I my mother? She'd like to believe she was better than that.

"Do you want to be held, or do you want space?" he offered.

Ari shook her head, her throat closing on the words, her mind in a flat spin. What did she want? Held in his arms, while she desperately tried to understand herself? Space to clear her mind...or worry more?

Bain turned to his side, settling Ari to the blanket beside him. His fingers stroked at the back of her neck, and he brushed his lips over hers.

"No," she pleaded. Her emotions and thoughts were rioting already. If they had sex again, it would only get worse.

"No sex," he promised.

Too late. Ari swallowed down a lump of emotion at that thought, her face burning in embarrassment.

"Just touch," he invited. "I moved too fast. I shouldn't have asked tonight."

His fingertips traced the lines of her face...then her throat. Ari planted one trembling hand on his chest, fingering the blond curls, stroking at his flat male nipples, bringing them to hard nubs.

In answer, he did the same for hers. Ari shifted against him, gasping at his renewed erection trailing along her inner thigh.

"Our clothes won't even come off next time," he vowed. "We'll just kiss...just touch."

She nodded, torn between her wants and the ghosts of her past.

Chapter Six

Ari waved at the departing school bus, her body humming in the memory of the night before. She'd woken several times, wet and wanting, on the verge of going to Bain's room. Even now, Ari wasn't sure if staying in her own room or going to his would have been the wrong choice.

Bain hadn't come down while the kids were still in the house, though she'd heard him moving around earlier. While Ari would like to take comfort in that fact, while she'd like to claim his absence had allowed her the peace to order her scattered thoughts, she knew it was a lie.

His absence made her worry all the more. Had he had second thoughts? Was he regretting it? Did he intend to apologize and move on? Her heart ached at the possibility.

She stepped inside the house and closed the door behind her, going still at the sight of Bain. He stood in the doorway between the living room and dining room, his feet shoulder-width apart and his arms loose at his sides. He was ready for action, and his expression announced that he hadn't reconsidered a thing.

The realization that she had to pass him to go anywhere else in the house, save the living room—and that room was equipped for a romp—brought her body to a nearly-painful edge of arousal.

Bain's gaze slid to her chest, no doubt noting her nipples pressing to the T-shirt. The urge to cover them passed quickly, though her face burned in the realization that he could catalog precisely how excited she was.

Why didn't I wear a bra this morning? Ari couldn't say whether it had been simple comfort or a hope for something more.

He licked his lips, as if savoring the memory of sucking those nipples the night before. His cock stirred, lengthening behind his jeans.

His hand came up, and he waited for Ari to cross the room and take it. She hesitated only a moment, then did so, her eyes slipping shut as his mouth covered hers.

The kiss was slow and deep, nothing like the frantic pace of the night before. Bain's arm crossed over her hip, drawing Ari closer. His lips parted from hers, but he kept them close, teasing her with more.

"Before I take you upstairs, I'm going to lay out the ground rules."

Her heart stuttered at the idea of them going upstairs. Beds were upstairs. Showers were.

"I won't be making love to you again for at least two days."

She stared at him, stunned by the pronouncement. Her body protested the wait, while her mind weighed it without a decisive answer on the subject.

Bain continued. "This time, the clothes stay on...every..." His lips feathered along her jawline to the sweet spot behind her ear. "Stitch," he breathed.

Ari nodded.

"I'm going to do my damnedest to get you to come fully clothed, but it will be fully clothed."

"And then? What are the other rules?"

"Tonight...if you want to progress..." He nipped at her earlobe.

I will. Ari didn't question it. Every touch made that two days sound excruciating.

Bain rolled his tongue around the shell of her ear. "The shirts come off. Tomorrow...if you want to—"

"I will." She blurted it out, tilting her head to encourage his play.

"Mouths and hands," he informed her. His breath played over wet flesh. "I'm going to eat you out until you can't stand it anymore. I'm going to finger-fuck you...and if you're willing–"

"You'll make love to me again?" *My God, is he really calling it that?*

"If you still feel the same way on Wednesday, we'll work our way up to that."

Her panties and jeans were already soaked with the proof of how much she wanted Wednesday to come. "What if I want to progress faster?"

"Huh uh," he chided gently. "We rushed last night, and you had regrets. If I see one moment of pain or regret, we move backward instead of forward."

At his pace! The thought was maddening. "And if I make you cream your jeans?" she challenged.

Bain drew his head back, his eyes hot in promise. "Please, do."

* * * *

That answer seemed to surprise her, but it was followed by a look of hunger that said they were going to continue.

Bain guided Ari up the stairs and into his bedroom, certain she'd be more at ease in his bed than in hers.

"Remove the shoes," he ordered. "Just the shoes...and socks, if you want to."

Ari toed off her tennis shoes, then pulled off her ankle socks and tucked them inside.

Bain sat on the edge of the mattress, wrapped his hands around her waist and drew Ari down beside him. He brought his lips to within an inch of hers.

"Close your eyes, Ari."

She hesitated and then complied.

He smiled at the plan taking shape from his indecisive—until now—mind. "It's just me and you, alone at lover's leap, sitting on the edge of the pickup bed."

Her breathing hitched and then smoothed.

Bain cupped his hand around her neck, bringing his mouth down on hers. There was nothing sweet and innocent about the kiss, nor did he want there to be. They were both experienced, and that's what Bain wanted to taste.

If her avid response was accurate, she agreed with that. He settled his free hand between her thighs, groaning at the heat radiating off of her, the damp proof that she wanted him.

Ari moved, leaving the kiss, easing away. Bain opened his eyes, his heart aching that she'd shied already. He was right; she wasn't ready for this, no matter how ready he was.

She wasn't shying from him. Ari was pushing herself along the bed, a sensual show that both invited him to follow and pleaded for more.

Bain turned to his hands and knees, stalking her along the mattress. Ari sank into the pillow, her gaze darting over him and her color high. Her legs were parted, one knee bent so her foot was flat on the surface of the bed, a clear indication of where she wanted him.

Crawling between her legs was a sweet agony. Visions of doing this naked, of tasting her, then thrusting inside at her climax, had him hard and needing sex he'd decreed he wouldn't be getting for another two days.

Her scent was sublime, and Bain paused to nuzzle at her, drinking it in greedily. Ari arched up off the bed in response, breathless little sounds escaping her. Encouraged, he stroked his tongue along her seam through her jeans. Her moan charged the air around them, lending the static-heavy ambiance that precedes a lightning strike to the encounter.

That's what it is. Even if this is all we do, the end is going to scorch.

Speaking of which, the heat against his lips cranked up a notch. Ari rolled her shoulders, shifting restlessly.

Bain dragged his teeth over the denim, smiling at her gasp and shiver. He moved up her body, nipping and nuzzling. Her hands fisted in his hair, and she tugged Bain up.

"Yes?" he breathed against the underside of a cotton-covered breast. He looked up at her, blowing hot puffs of air over her nipple.

Ari licked her lips, tugging upward again.

He laid a single lick over her nipple. "Later. When the shirts go." Bain didn't question that she intended to take that step; given the option, he felt certain she'd already have them half-off.

And regret it ten minutes later. Not this time.

Her thighs tightened around his waist, and Bain forced them open, his hand lingering on her inner thigh. He eased up her body.

Ari tipped her hips up, pleading silently for what she wanted. The first thrust of his cock against her wrenched a moan from her.

Her hand delved beneath his T-shirt, and Bain sucked in his breath in surprise.

"No. The clothes—"

"Won't come off," she breathed. Her wicked fingers went to work on his nipples. Ari stared at him, waiting for his answer.

At the pinch on his nipple, Bain moved, flipping to his back and pulling Ari over him. "Ride me," he ordered.

He didn't have to say it twice. Ari ground against him, her eyes closing, her back arching.

Bain dragged her shirt from her jeans, seeking out her already pebbled nipples beneath. "My mouth is watering," he confided.

Ari moved faster, driving herself to a climax he wanted to taste. The idea of licking and sucking the flavor off her nether lips had him groaning. It would be at least a day before he'd get that.

She made a concerted effort at stroking him off, visibly taking his measure. Bain started to give her his dimensions, in comparison to David, then stopped in the realization that the last thing he wanted her thinking about was her dead husband.

Still, he reveled in the fact that he was thicker...and slightly shorter than David had been. David had bragged about how he bottomed out painfully in Ari whenever things got heated.

Even then, Bain had wanted to knock out teeth. The fact that David took pleasure in causing Ari pain during sex was revolting on several levels. The fact that he gauged his manhood as secure by being too large for his wife's comfort only proved he was no man. Not in Bain's book.

Memories of her enjoyment the night before spelled the end of his control. Bain surrendered to the sweet sensation with a roar.

Afterward, Ari lay over him, seemingly stunned. Bain reached between them and traced lazy little circles over her soaked seam.

Ari jerked against him, a ragged shout escaping her. Her hands tightened on his shoulders, and her thighs trembled and jumped against his hand.

"Mmm...came again, didn't you?" Just the thought of it had his voice ragged and his cock complaining for more. He wanted to feel her sheath contracting around him, feel her milking the cum out of him.

"Yes," she gasped out.

Bain turned her beneath him again, groaning at her legs coming up to cradle him. "You are so responsive."

Ari looked like she was about to argue that point. Instead, she smiled.

"What's so funny?" he asked.

"We're going to have a lot of laundry to do if we keep this up."

His cock jerked against her, and Ari's eyes slid shut.

"Oh, I'm up." There was little question he was going to stay up.

Chapter Seven

Bain took his time getting ready to go down to the den. He'd been pouncing on Ari so far, always to the scene before her, always initiating what they did. It was time to give her a little space and see what she would do when he let her have time to initiate.

He waited a full five minutes after he heard her tuck Matt and Josie in and head down the stairs to follow her.

The house was much quieter than it had been even days earlier, when there'd been five children in the house instead of three. It was starting to feel downright empty, and the word was that Mike would be arriving to pick up Matt within a day or two.

The den door swung open, and he looked for her. The view stopped his heart for a moment. Ari sat on the futon, the button down shirt fully unbuttoned, giving him just a peek at her breasts.

"Bain?"

He swallowed the lump in his throat, shut the door, and ambled toward her. Bain sank to the futon beside her and reached out to pull the shirt open.

Ari closed the shirt over her chest and crossed her arms. The abrupt change was like ice water in his face, and Bain stared at her, seeking answers.

A shy little smile curved her lips. "I'll show you mine, if you show me yours."

That brought a smile back to his face. "I never thought I'd hear that one again," he admitted.

"I never thought I'd be taken to lovers' leap again," she countered.

"Touché, my dear. Touché." Bain stripped off his T-shirt and let it fall to the floor.

Ari's gaze slid down his chest like a caress, examining every inch of his uncovered flesh.

He wanted to tease her that he'd shown his and it was her turn to show hers, but that went against his experiment. Instead, he waited to see what she'd do next.

Her arms loosened, and she planted her hands on his thighs. Ari leaned toward him, her lips parting to his.

Bain didn't hesitate. The hours of veiled glances and stolen touches once the kids got home from school had been pure torture. It was going to be even worse when his leave was up next week, and he'd be separated from her for ten hour shifts, five or six days a week.

The thought was enough to break his control. Bain slid the shirt over her shoulders and down her arms. Ari left the kiss long enough to shuck it to the mattress. Then she was straddling him, chest to chest and mouth to mouth with him.

Bain wrapped her in his arms, reveling in the sensation. How many times had he dreamed of holding her like this? Too many to count.

They shifted, turned, and sank to the mattress. Ari felt right beneath him, just as he'd always known she would.

She grumbled something against his lips, and Bain raised his head.

"Too much weight?" he asked.

"No, but not enough room to move."

He smiled at her candor and turned to his side, drawing Ari along. Despite the fact that she'd claimed the weight wasn't an issue, she breathed easier at the change.

Bain cupped one breast in his hand, rubbing a thumb over her nipple. "Yeah. This is definitely better."

Ari licked her lips. "I have to agree."

Her hands started at his shoulders, investigating the lines of his body. Her fingertips tangled in the curls on his chest, making his cock demand more.

He took her lead, smoothing a hand down the curves of her body, taking his time, memorizing every inch of silky skin. Bain was glad he'd decided to let her set the pace.

Ari sought out the scar from an electrical burn he'd gotten working on a panel after flooding. She didn't have to comment that he'd gotten it in the years they'd been apart. That would have been all too obvious to her.

If she looked at me intently then. He wasn't sure whether that was accurate. *And now is not the time to obsess over it.*

Exploration of hands gave way to exploration of mouths. Ari started with the scar, her lips tracing the edges. Her hot breath rained down on one nipple, and Bain groaned.

As if taking that as encouragement, she licked then sucked. The pleasure knifed through him, bringing his hips up hard against hers. Her teeth raked at the peak of his nipple, and he gasped out a ragged "yes." Bain cupped her head, reining in the urge to drag her mouth up to his.

Maybe something in his movements or sounds let her know what he wanted. Ari worked her way up his chest to his throat. She raked her teeth again and then moved on. Up his throat. Down the line of his chin. Up to his lips.

His body in a riot, Bain crushed his lips to hers. She parted hers with a moan, inviting him in. The kiss was hard and hot, and Ari's hands inched down his chest and stomach to the button on his jeans.

I'll let her. I swear to God, if she initiates this, I'll let her. Forget the damned plan.

Ari showed no signs of stopping, and his heart raced in excitement, as she pulled at the button.

The sound of the doorbell shocked Bain out of the moment, and he cursed fluently.

Ari raised her head and looked toward the closed door. "Who would show up now?" she complained.

He slid off her and snagged his T-shirt. "I don't know, but I'm going to find out." He dragged his shirt on and let it pool sloppily over his erection.

Frustration driving him, Bain stormed toward the door. The doorbell rang again, and he yanked it open without checking the peep hole.

The kid on the other side jumped at the move. He gaped at Bain, going wide-eyed.

"Well?" Bain demanded.

"S-sorry. I was looking for Aurora Evans."

"At this time of night?" He surveyed the kid's rumpled fatigues with distaste.

His cheeks darkened. "I know. Matt's probably already asleep, but... I just got in, and..." He groaned, looking tortured.

Bain's anger dissipated. "Mike?"

He fumbled his wallet out of his front pocket and showed his military ID.

"Get in here." Bain cleared the way and waved him into the living room.

Mike hoisted a sea bag onto his shoulder, ambled to the love seat, and sank into it. "Sorry. Honest. I don't know what I was thinking."

"I do." Bain knew all too well how hard it had been to walk away from Ari once he'd found her. "Do you have a place to stay tonight?" Mike had come here on the rush, and Bain was half-certain the young man hadn't planned any of this in advance.

He's so young. Indecently young. If he's as old as nineteen, I'd be amazed.

His expression was pure panic.

No idea.

"I can't take Matt to the billet they gave me."

"No. You can't do that," he agreed. Though the military hospitals had to remind pregnant and newly delivered female service members that fairly often.

"I can call another cab, I guess. Go to the billet...or take him to the lodge, until they give us a place tomorrow." His tone was uncertain.

And he should be. "There's no saying the lodge has an opening tonight. They fill up quick with people transferring in and out."

"Oh." His disappointment gnawed at Bain.

"We have a futon in the den." That pronouncement came from Ari.

Bain looked over his shoulder at her and nodded his agreement. He'd been working his way to the same decision.

Mike fingered the edge of his sea bag. Just when Bain thought he would beg off or claim it would be too much trouble or something equally stupid, he mumbled his thanks.

Ari smiled. "Spend the night and have breakfast with us. By then, the housing office should be open."

He met her eyes, opened his mouth, and shut it again. "Thank you isn't enough."

She sighed. "Bain, can you get him some fresh sheets and a blanket?" she asked.

"Sure." Probably better that than having a horny young guy, fresh from the field, getting a lungful of the scent they'd surely left on the blanket he'd placed there earlier in the day.

Bain took the stairs two at a time and turned toward the linen closet next to the hall bath. He paused with his hand on the door handle and looked up to find Lea, glaring at him from the doorway to her room.

He was well aware of what he looked like. His T-shirt was rumpled and untucked. His hair was mussed, and he might even have an abrasion of Ari's teeth on his neck.

"Matt's brother is here and staying the night," he told her. That accomplished, Bain grabbed a stack of full-sized sheets and pillowcase, a pillow, and a blanket and headed for the stairs.

To his surprise, Lea didn't offer any comment.

Changing the sheets and airing the room didn't take long. Bain ditched the blanket they'd been using in the washer and started it running. Then he returned to Mike and Ari.

She'd taken a seat on the couch and folded her legs under her.

Mike had his elbows on his knees, his head bowed. He looked prematurely aged, and Bain felt a pang of sympathy for him.

"That's why I joined up. You know?"

"Your parents?" Ari asked.

"And Matt. The day I saw the list of the dead from..." He swallowed what might have been a sob. "They were all gone. Dead and unidentified somewhere or missing or lost or whatever Matt was, I had no one left. I wanted to make them pay. If joining up was the only way to do that..." His voice went surer at that. "Well, I joined up. They weren't asking questions. As long as you were willing to fight, everything else was a rubber stamp."

Ari looked up at Bain, clearly tortured by what she was hearing.

"Bed's ready, Mike," Bain announced. "Looks like you can use some sleep."

"A week of it," he quipped. He stumbled to his feet.

Bain guided him toward the den. "How about eight or nine hours?" he offered.

"Heaven." Mike scrubbed a hand down his face. "I don't know how to be a dad," he admitted.

"Then don't be his dad," Ari suggested. "I'm not his mom. Bain isn't his dad. Be his big brother. All he needs is someone willing to be the adult for him."

"And don't be afraid to give him E.M.I., when he needs it," Bain instructed.

Mike's brow furrowed. "You gave him E.M.I.?"

Bain chuckled. "You will never see kids move so fast. Guaranteed."

He staggered through the door, dropped his sea bag, and collapsed to the futon without so much as removing his boots. "How do I–"

"Tomorrow," Ari ordered. "It's time to sleep."

Mike mumbled something in return.

Bain shut the door with a sigh.

"I know," Ari whispered. "It's like having four kids in the house again. He's so young."

"He'll do fine."

"With a little help, I think he will," she agreed.

Chapter Eight

Ari looked up from the stove at the rush of feet into the kitchen. Josie and Matt jockeyed for position, each of them trying to get the master chair at the head of the table.

"Matt," Ari called out.

He looked up at her, giving Josie the opportunity she needed to slip into the chair and cheer victory. Matt scowled at Ari.

"I have a surprise for you," she promised.

One brow went up. "Really?"

"Yep. Why don't you go check in the den?"

Bain ambled into the kitchen, turning to watch Matt charge for the door to the den. He smiled and waited for Matt's response.

The door opened, and Matt went still. After a minute, he gasped out his brother's name.

"Hey, buddy," Mike grumbled.

"Mike!"

Their voices rose in an excited chatter, and Bain crossed the room to Ari's side. She handed off Josie's plate of eggs and bacon to him and planted a kiss on his cheek. Bain delivered the plate, came back for the next two Ari had ready, and tipped his head to Lea on the way to the table with them.

Lea peeked into the den on her way across the room and headed for the stove to pick up her own plate. "Morning, Mom," she offered brightly. "I take it everything is going well with Matt and his brother?"

She nodded just as Mike and Matt came out of the den. The older nodded to her, then followed his brother to the half bath. They were back in moments and settled in at the table with Lea and Josie.

Mike surveyed the plate set for him, nearly salivating. "This is great. Thanks again." He didn't wait for a reply to dig in.

Ari handed Bain's plate to him and picked up her own. They walked to the table and took seats together. Lea's eyes narrowed at the move, then she went back to her breakfast.

After a few bites, Ari addressed Mike. "Do you want to take Matt with you today or let him go to school like normal? You'll get more done without him, but he won't pay much attention in school if he goes."

He seemed to consider it carefully. "I know I should make him go to school–"

"Mi-ike," Matt whined.

"I believe you said E.M.I. was the answer to that?" his brother inquired, without missing a beat.

He's going to do just fine. Ari offered a nod and took another bite of her eggs.

Matt pouted and pushed the eggs around his plate, no doubt envisioning a long, boring day of school.

Mike sighed. "To be honest, I don't want to let him go to school. I think we both deserve one day off."

"That makes sense," Ari replied, sensing that he needed reassurance that it was a solid choice for a parent to make.

Matt smiled widely.

"But don't count on it often, twerp," he cautioned.

Bain swallowed a mouthful of orange juice and set his glass down. "After breakfast, Matt can show you where my shower is. Get cleaned up, and I'll help Matt pack his gear."

Mike winced and then forced his expression to smooth.

Ari motioned to him. "We're not cutting you loose, Mike. You're going to need advice...and a little help. You can arrange for the before-school program at the school and have Matt dropped off here after school. We can work something out for covering your duty days. We'll get you back on your feet."

"I don't even know how to cook eggs," he admitted.

"I like cereal," Matt piped up.

"Not too much sugar," Bain inserted.

"You'll learn," Ari assured him. "It's not as difficult as it looks."

"Oh yeah? I've caught a stove on fire," Mike grumbled.

Ari opened her mouth to answer.

"Boiling water," he qualified.

She winced. "Maybe we should build cooking classes into that schedule."

Bain chuckled. "Probably. I'd call that safety training."

"Got a fire extinguisher?" Mike quipped, his mood lightening.

"Two."

* * * *

Bain parked in the drive and let himself out of the car, his heart pounding. After Lea had left for her bus, he'd helped Matt pack while Mike showered and changed. Ari had put Josie on her bus, and Bain had provided a ride for Mike and Matt to P.S.D.. From there, it would be a short walk to the housing office and a matter of no more than eight blocks to whichever apartment they were assigned to. All of that accomplished, he was headed home to Ari.

Arousal from their aborted evening sang in his veins. There was no question that he would have given in and abandoned his grand plan if they'd been uninterrupted for much longer. If Mike had been even five minutes later, he would have had to wait for Bain to put more than his shirt back on.

Hell, he would have waited for me to finish. What a mess that would have been. Lea would have ended up answering the door for the young man and probably reveled in disturbing them to announce Mike's arrival.

Bain opened the door, stepped inside, and swung it shut behind him. He reached for the lock, scanning the area for signs of–

Ari's push against his chest shocked him, and Bain took an involuntary step backward, colliding with the door. Her mouth closed on his, and her hands went to work on his jeans.

Hell yes! They'd only indulged in the den and his bedroom so far. If her urgency was any indication, it was going to be the living room this morning.

His jeans opened, Ari dragged them to his upper thighs. Her hand circled his cock and started stroking. Her mouth left his, and she sank to her knees between his spread ankles.

"Aurora can suck a golf ball through fifty feet of garden hose."

Bain shivered at the memory. How many times had David claimed his wife's mouth was her best asset?

How many times had he gloated about her prowess and her willingness to suck him?

Too damned many for my sanity.

His sanity took another blow as she sucked him into the heat of her mouth. Ari took half his length on the first stroke, retreated, and came back a little deeper.

"Oh...fuck," he breathed. "So good."

Her mouth wasn't just good. It was mind-altering.

He knew better than to lock his knees to stay upright; that was a sure recipe for passing out. Since he wasn't certain he'd stay conscious through the coming climax, making it less likely wasn't a good idea.

Ari moaned around his length, moving him in and out, faster and deeper. It was a challenge, he was sure.

Bain grasped the doorknob, his knees shaking. *I have to stay on my feet.*

She started circling her tongue along the sensitive lower ridge of his cock. The suction increased, making his vision blur. Then she was moving again.

"Fuck!" Bain ground his teeth, trying to hold off his climax. That being a lost cause, he blurted out a warning. "I'm going to come."

He knew she'd swallowed for David, but Ari had done a lot of things for her husband that Bain knew she really didn't want to do. If this was one more, he vowed not to be too disappointed.

That's a fucking lie.

I still owe her the chance to pull away. "Ari, if you don't want to–"

She took him deep—nearly to the root. Her mouth worked at his cock, massaging him over.

Bain grasped the back of her head with his free hand and let loose with a roar. Cum raced up his length in a soothing flow, taking the mounting tension with it. It had been less than two days since he'd had sex with her, less than twelve hours since he'd come, and he came like he'd just returned from a three-month deployment.

Of course. It's Ari. Had he ever doubted what sex would be like between them?

Never.

His cock spasmed as she swallowed, and he groaned in pleasure. *If she did this the first night, Lea would have known then. No one in the house would have missed my reaction.*

Bain let his head drop back and panted, his knees still shaking. He stroked at her hair, hissing out a breath at the stroking of her tongue up the veins and over the head. Her mouth retreated, and she seemed to wait for a response from him.

* * * *

He was silent and still for so long, Ari felt her nerves jumping.

Just let him do something different than David used to. It had taken her only a day with Bain to decide that her late husband had been an exceedingly selfish lover. She'd suspected it for some time, but with no comparison, Ari couldn't be sure. Even in the earliest days of their relationship, David had never been half as giving as Bain was.

"Oh, God, that was good."

Her heart sank. Maybe the assumption was universal to men.

"Thank you."

That was all it took to prove him a more attractive lover than David was. He appreciated what she did for him. He didn't expect it.

I knew that. Bain had asked if she wanted to swallow. He'd given her the cue to back off, if she didn't want to.

He didn't force my head down, either. He let me choose my pace and depth. There was something appealing in that. Maybe there was a reason other women didn't seem so put off by giving oral sex.

"Come up here." Bain's voice was gravelly, deep.

The sound was enough to make her wet. Ari pushed to her feet, acutely aware that she was nude beneath his T-shirt.

Bain cupped his hands beneath her buttocks and drew her to his body. His eyes were darkened and dilated. His breath was hot against her lips.

He kissed her. After a moment of shock, she started participating.

He pulled back. "Problem?"

"No." *Not at all. David never wanted to kiss me afterward. He hadn't wanted to taste himself in my mouth.* There was something arousing in being kissed. Maybe it was the novelty of it.

Ari didn't question it. She closed on his lips again.

Bain's hands slid beneath the T-shirt and up the curve of her ass. He drew away from the kiss again. "You are doing this for me again."

Keeping up with his subject changes wasn't as easy as it usually was. "Sucking you?"

"I wouldn't mind that, but I meant wearing one of my shirts with nothing underneath."

She darkened. It had been an impetuous move, one she'd never seriously contemplated with David. He'd been a fan of lacy lingerie. He would have scowled at the sight of her in one of his shirts; David would no doubt have found it completely unappealing. On some level, the fact that Bain liked both extremes surprised her.

Bain's eyes darkened. "Problem?" he asked again.

"No. No problem." Ari fought to come up with anything to say.

He saved her the trouble. "I am going to raise the shirt just a bit and slide my cock inside."

The visual was too much for her, and Ari parted her thighs, inviting him in. It was presumptuous, considering his grand plan of a long, slow build-up, but she'd been just as presumptuous the night before, and it might have paid off if Mike hadn't shown up when he had. Bain certainly hadn't called a halt at her move to open his jeans. She still wondered how far he would have let her go.

"Not now," he amended. "Tomorrow night. In my room."

"Your room?" *At night?* He hadn't suggested that before.

"I could come to yours, but I figured you'd be more comfortable in mine."

Farther away from the girls. She nodded dumbly.

"Maybe we should start with that tonight."

"Your room?" she asked for qualification.

"Mmmm hmmm. My room. My bed."

"What should I wear?" She hoped the answer would be one of his shirts. She prayed he intended to lift it just a little and end this torture.

"A pair of jeans I can peel off your body nice and slow?"

Ari swore she was wet to the knees. He was driving her crazy with his teasing. *And he hasn't even touched me yet.*

"You like that. Don't you?"

"The idea of you doing it or you telling me that you're going to?"

His head cocked to one side, and he stared down at her. "You like both." He didn't question it.

"Hell yes, I do."

One hand left her ass and reappeared, combing through her curls to her clit. Ari shifted her hips to urge him to her slit. She was empty and wanted filled, however he was willing to.

"Mmmm... So wet for me. You do like hearing what I'm going to do to you."

She nodded.

His fingers played along the seam, then just inside. "I like hearing what you want me to do to you."

"I want your cock inside me." It was out there before she considered how vulnerable the admission would make her.

His cock jerked against her belly, leaving a wet trail that said she'd struck gold by saying it. "You have to wait just a little longer for that."

Ari squeezed her eyes shut, needing more than what he was doing.

"The waiting is driving you as crazy as it's driving me."

"I hope so."

His index and middle fingers speared deep, wrenching a moan from her. His finger fucking was slow and purposeful, and her toes curled into the rug in response.

"It is driving me nuts, Ari. Now, since you like hearing it, I am going to make you come in my arms. Then I am going to take you over to that couch, spread your legs, and eat every drop of the musk that's coating your thighs."

Ari grasped at his arms, needing support for her shaking legs.

"After that, we'll head up to my bed."

"And what's going to happen there?" she asked.

"What do you want to have happen there? Within the rules set for us already," he qualified.

Forming words was even more difficult than forming thoughts. "Sixty–"

His stroking fingers went into overdrive, forcing her into a kinetic climax. Ari shouted in surprise, her head rocking back as her muscles tensed and relaxed wildly.

Bain scooped her up in his arms and started walking.

"Where are we going?" she asked weakly.

"Where did I promise?"

The couch cushions teasing at the backs of her thighs answered before her mind could sort the conversation.

"Oh...yes." *To anything he suggests.*

* * * *

"Hey, Bain," Lea called out, seemingly distracted. "Seen my mom?"

"Taking a shower." To make how they'd spent the day less obvious, he was sure. "She should be down in a few."

"Only if she's been in there for half an hour."

Bain turned to her, one brow arching in puzzlement.

Lea looked up from the paper in her hand, locking on him. "Uh...she sort of likes long, hot showers."

That was information he intended to use.

Whatever hunger might have shown on his face was lost on Lea. She was already reading the paper in her hand again.

"What do you have there?" he asked, curious.

Lea folded it, her spine stiffening. "Why do you have to know?"

"I don't *have* to know anything. I was just–"

"You're not my mom, Bain. It's none of your business."

It was time to take the little tigress by the tail. "Just because I'm not your dad doesn't mean I don't care, Lea."

His answer seemed to confuse her. Her brow furrowed, and she blinked several times, as if searching for something elusive.

"Lea–"

"You actually care about school stuff?" she blurted out.

"Sure. Why wouldn't I?"

She didn't answer that.

"I'm sure your dad would–"

"Why would he care about school stuff?"

Good God, she's serious. "Why wouldn't he?"

"It's not a guy thing. Ya know?"

Bain considered that. "No, I don't think I know what you mean."

Lea rolled her eyes. "You go out to work. Right?"

He nodded, trying to follow her logic.

"You back up Mom on discipline, but you don't discipline."

"Without Ari's permission? Of course not."

"Right, because that's a mom thing." Lea stated it as if it was a foregone conclusion.

Bain took a calming breath. "So what all do you consider mom things?"

Lea settled on a chair and threw her legs over the arm. "School stuff, doctor stuff, discipline, keeping the calendar... You know, birthday parties and stuff like that."

"That it?" he asked, still trying to dissect the fact that David had been so uninvolved.

"Well, you know...housework and her own work."

"Dishes and floors?" Something told him it wasn't that simple.

Lea scowled at him. "Is that all *you* do around the house? Of course not. There's the snow-blowing and the yard and...fixing things, laundry... House work. I help, of course. I mean...somebody should, right?"

Curiosity got the better of him. "And where was your dad?" Why wasn't he doing any of it? What was his input, besides an outside job and the money it brought in?

She shrugged. "At work, I guess."

"All the time?"

"Pretty near. He wasn't home much."

Bain worked at that. It made a certain amount of sense, he supposed. Even in the Navy, David had invented reasons not to be home. He'd go to a party and leave Ari caring for Lea. He'd go out with the guys while she was home cooking dinner for him, without warning her he wouldn't be coming home. How often was he home and doing the husband and father routine?

Not often. That was one of the things he'd pointed out to Ari when he'd tried to convince her to leave David's sorry ass.

What didn't make sense was why Ari put up with fifteen years of it. Bain just couldn't fathom a woman being ignored that long and swallowing the gross neglect.

Then Lea dropped the bomb. "That's why she was leaving him. Didn't you know that?"

No. Bain hadn't known that. He leaned against the wall, needing balance he seemed to have misplaced. "They were divorcing?"

She smiled weakly. "That was the plan."

"And what happened to that plan?" Why had she stayed with him?

"Mom got the phone call."

"Phone call?" Why did nothing Lea say make sense?

"The one telling her she had fifteen minutes to grab me and what she could and be on the road."

Bain ambled to the couch and sank into it. "That must have freaked her." What sane woman wouldn't have been frantic at such a call?

Lea chuckled. "Nah. She'd been expecting that call for over a year." Her smile disappeared. "Now the massacre at Refugee Ridge... *That* freaked her."

"You saw it?" He could hardly imagine the kids seeing something like that.

"Me? No. Mom wouldn't let me have the binoculars. She didn't watch for long, either. Just long enough to..." She swallowed hard, looking away to the windows. "Then we bagged with the supplies on our backs. Good thing Mom insisted we always be ready to run." She paused, chewing at her lower lip for a long moment. "That's how we made it out of the house in ten minutes. She was already packed."

"Then she knew what your dad was doing."

Lea sighed. "As little as they talked, it's highly unlikely."

Which brought them full circle. Bain wasn't David, and it seemed proving the differences would be fairly simple. "So what's the school stuff you brought home, Lea?"

She turned her head, considering him. "I know what this is...and you don't have to try so hard, Bain."

He found forming a sentence difficult. "What do you think this is?"

"My dad always hinted that there was a...a history between you and Mom."

I wish.

"I know you two were together when Mike got here. I'm not blind or deaf. The looks you shoot each other...especially this morning..." She blushed. "I haven't seen Mom this happy in years."

Bain winced, half in the realization that Lea knew and half in discomfort at the idea of Ari so unhappy.

"It's okay with me," she assured him. "I like seeing Mom happy, you know."

He stared at her, caught between laughter and disbelief. "I know."

"But you make her cry, and I'll come up with a weapon and make you pay for it. I hate it when she cries."

Bain didn't give in to the urge to laugh. Lea was serious, and he wouldn't risk making her think he didn't take this seriously. "That's a deal, because I don't intend on making Ari cry."

Lea nodded grimly. "I'll take that as a promise."

"I don't break them," he assured her. "Now, what's this school stuff?"

She hesitated. "Swimming. I want to join the swim team."

"Sounds good to me. When's your first meet?"

Chapter Nine

Ari strode toward Bain's room, fresh from the shower and half lost in thought. If Lea's hint that she would like her own room...Ari's room, was any indication, her daughter was banking on Ari not spending a lot of time in that room. She was probably right about that.

For as long as whatever is happening continues. The idea of it ending was rather disheartening, and Ari forced her mind back to Lea instead of dwelling over where she'd choose to sleep when that happened, if she surrendered her room to Lea now.

There'd been no tension over the subject, just a matter-of-fact comment from her insightful daughter. Ari wasn't sure why that shocked her. She'd made a habit of being truthful with Lea, which was one of the reasons her daughter was so mature for her age.

Lea knew sex between Ari and David had been less than stellar. She knew the faults in both of her parents that had driven the marriage into the dust. Lea knew Ari had every intention of leaving David behind and seeking something better for herself, even before he ended up dead.

Ari smiled at that. Bain was decidedly better than David had been. She cursed herself again for her bad decision making all those years ago.

She stepped through the open door to his room and closed it behind her, lost in thought of how to give Lea her own room...without that room being too close to Bain's. She mused that she could move into the room Matt had been using, and he could use the den any night he was–

A hand covered her mouth, and an arm encircled her waist, locking her to a very male chest. Ari stiffened at the abrupt move.

"Shhh... Listen," Bain whispered.

Memories of their scare in the mountains had her shivering.

He guided her toward the bed. "Down," he breathed into her ear.

She complied, biting back a moan at what came next. Bain covered her, his cock nestling to the curve of her buttocks, setting her senses in a spin much as it had that night.

This time, we aren't surrounded by children and his men. This time, there aren't Federalist soldiers a few dozen yards away.

Bain didn't force her flat beneath him, as he had that night. He rested on one elbow, using his free hand to play at her breasts through the single layer of the button-down shirt she wore. After a moment, he slid his hand away from her mouth.

"You wanted me that night," he guessed.

"Yes." She'd more than wanted him; it had taken all of her self-control not to wiggle against him in invitation.

"Do you want me now? Are you wet for me?"

"Oh, yes." Just the thought of it was enough to get her aching for him.

Bain eased his hips up slightly, forcing his hand between Ari and the mattress. His fingers played at her through her jeans, and he hummed a low note. "Very wet," he purred. "Very inviting."

Ari cycled her hips back and forth, riding his fingertips.

"Will you do that while I'm inside you, Ari?"

"If you're going to be inside me." The wait was going to drive her crazy.

His hand retreated, and she moaned, wondering what he intended. The button and zipper on her jeans opening announced that it would be skin-to-skin. Bain went to his knees, working the jeans and panties beneath as far down her thighs as his own legs allowed.

Fingers stroking at and then between her slit had Ari gasping for breath and rising against him. Two thick digits delved inside, and she fisted the sheet.

His voice rumbled over her raw nerves. "I'm not walking away this time," he promised. "Say the word, and I'm here for the whole show."

"I don't want you to walk away." She didn't. A cold shower or self-stimulation certainly wasn't going to calm this fervor.

"I mean it, Ari. I'm talking a serious commitment here." There was something she vaguely recognized as a warning in that.

"Bain, please–"

He started finger fucking her, making rational thought nearly impossible.

"Do you understand me, Ari?"

Some remote corner of her mind worked out that he was proposing something longer-term than a couple of nights of sex. Since Ari couldn't come up with an arrangement she'd balk at—including sex slave—she nodded her agreement.

She was abruptly empty. Ari's pleas for more ended at the sound of Bain's zipper sliding down. Her heart skipped in surprise and excitement.

"Yes, Bain," she breathed her encouragement. *Oh please, let him be planning to finish it, this time.* If he backed off and made her wait for the morning...

Tomorrow. Midnight is in three hours plus small change. If it comes to that, I'm not taking no for an answer.

But Bain wasn't waiting. His hands circled her hips and lifted slightly; his length slid home. Ari tried to stifle her cry into the mattress, but much of it escaped into the room around them.

"That's right," he instructed. "Show me what you want."

Ari shifted her hips, forcing him in and out. He matched her rhythm, taking her deep.

Deep and not bottoming out. God, that feels good.

"You're sleeping here, tonight," he informed her. "You'll be sleeping here every night...or both of us in your room, but since the master bath is here, it makes more sense to stay here."

"To—together," she managed.

"You said you understood me," he replied patiently.

Ari nodded her agreement, fisting her hand tighter in the sheet, gasping as her push back forced him to the hilt in her. *And still not bottoming out.*

Bain panted out something that sounded like a curse. "Tomorrow morning, I'll get up with the kids," he continued. "When I take Josie to the bus, you'll start on a shower. Start...don't finish without me."

Visions of Bain stepping naked into the spray had her at the edges of climax.

He groaned. "I'm glad you agree."

"Oh, I agree." Ari was honest enough to admit she'd agree to almost anything that meant more of this. *I was an idiot to refuse him all those years ago.*

As if punctuating that thought, Bain increased his pace, taking her hard and fast.

That ended the discussion. Forming coherent words through sounds of mindless pleasure being virtually impossible, Ari settled for urging him on in a more primal manner.

He outlasted her, though not by much. His cock pulsed jets of hot cum against sensitized, contracting bands of muscle. Their sharp sounds of climax created a rich symphony in the semi-darkness.

In a blur of motion, Bain's weight was over her, pinning her to the bed from shoulders to knees. His bare foot nestled beneath hers caught her attention. In some manner, it was more intimate than the rest combined, including his cock softening within her.

Bain's lips pressed to her temple. "Say something," he requested.

Ari sighed. "I don't think I've recovered enough to make sense."

A deep chuckle stirred the dark waves of hair over her cheeks. "You sound like you're making sense to me."

"That's only because you're still befuddled, too." A smile pulled her lips up.

Bain didn't respond to that. He eased out of her, then settled to the mattress, turning Ari into his arms. The buttons on her shirt slid open to his busy fingers.

Ari arched against him. "Bain?"

"I think I like being befuddled. It's a state I'd like to spend a lot of time in."

The inference hit her libido full force. Ari pushed up at his T-shirt, speeding him on.

* * * *

Bain forced his mind to function. There were answers he needed, answers he'd promised himself he'd get tonight, but her lips pressed to his chest weren't helping.

"Why didn't you tell me you were getting divorced?" he managed to ask, his voice thick.

She went still, a gasp puffing over his abdomen, ruffling the curls that bisected the lines of muscle. "Wh—what?"

Bain eased her up until she rested belly to belly with him. "Were you?" He sure as hell hoped so. He hoped Lea was being honest, and that Ari wasn't still hung up on David.

"Yeah." Her voice came out squeaky, and Ari cleared her throat before continuing. "It might have lasted another month or two. After that, I would have left him for good." She barely seemed to breathe.

He pressed a kiss to her forehead, blessing his luck. "Why didn't you tell me?"

Ari didn't answer with more than a shrug.

"Ari..." Words failed him. Didn't she trust him?

"You were right. All right?" There was an edge of tears threatening in that.

Bain held her tighter. "What, Ari? What was I right about?"

A slight tremor worked its way through her. He felt it from shoulder to feet.

Realization dropped the floor out of his stomach. "About David." He didn't question it. "Way back then...what I said about David."

"I made the wrong choice. I know it."

Bain squeezed his eyes shut, his heart pounding. Half of him wanted to comfort her; the other half wanted to crow in triumph.

The age-old question still burned at him. "Why did you choose him? Why David and not me?"

"Anything worth having is work," she whispered.

He didn't question her. Ari was working her way up to something, something that was twelve years in the making. He had to give her room to reach it at her own pace.

"My mother would walk away any time it got tough... Just drop everything and throw it all away, find someone new, make promises...until it got tough again." She hesitated.

Bain considered that. "And what did that do to you?" he mused aloud.

Her breathing hitched. "What would it do to Lea?"

"You're not your mother," he offered. *That was lame. Why can't I come up with something better than that?*

"Sometimes... Sometimes, there's nothing to fight for," she stammered out.

Bain pressed his forehead to hers. "Sometimes, there is. I was wrong, too."

"Wha–"

He flatted his hand to the back of her head and kissed her. Ari pressed against him, damp pubic curls tangling, his cock stirring. Bain went back to work on her shirt. Their mouths parted, meshed, parted again.

In between, he breathed an answer. "I shouldn't have kept my mouth shut. I should have said something, before you married him."

Ari's hands slid under his T-shirt. "Maybe you should have."

Chapter Ten

November 5th

Ari was in the shower first. She wasn't first every morning, but she was restless this morning, which meant she'd woken well before the alarm went off.

She didn't question why she was so squirrelly. She hated doctors with a passion. Any time she had to go to one, it was a major source of stress for her.

Which is hardly good for my health. Ari had chided herself about that many times, but there was no reasoning with an unreasonable fear. Doctors were hers.

The draft of cold air gave her only a moment's notice that Bain was about to join her. His larger body blocked the stream of water and left her with a fine mist of water instead of the pounding spray. Her move to turn to him ended with his hands cupping her breasts and kneading them lightly. She licked her lips, and leaned into him for more.

"Oh, I missed this."

"Touching my breasts? I think you fondled one for half the night," she teased.

"Showering with you, smart ass." But there was no bite of displeasure in the answer.

"That's only been about a week."

"Almost two. You've been sleeping in." He pressed his cock to her back, making a silent show of how much he missed it.

"Mmmm... Sorry. I've been stuffed up." Ari waved a hand at the shower head. "Hot water helps a bit."

His hand stopped massaging. "Sick?" The concern in his voice was impossible to miss.

"No, but you know me. If I don't get the congestion cleared up, I will be." Already, Ari was having bouts of dizziness that came along with congestion behind the eardrums.

"Doctor." It was a bark of order. From David, it would have annoyed her. Coming from Bain—knowing he wasn't just reacting to the idea of her being sick imposing on him—it was rather endearing.

"Already set up for today," she assured him. Ari pressed back against his cock, trying to move him to a more enjoyable subject.

His hand skated down her stomach and over her mound to her slit. He stroked idly along the length of it. "I didn't have to threaten you?"

"Someone told me to learn to take care of myself," she hinted.

His fingers thrust inside, bringing Ari to her toes. Pleasure knifed through her at the stimulation.

"I think that deserves a reward."

She planted her hands on the shower wall. "You know what reward I want."

Bain growled, his fingers retreating. "When you say things like that, all my plans go out the window."

Her half-formed reply morphed to a moan at the sensation of his cock pressing to her nether lips and maneuvering inside. Ari raised her foot and planted it against a low shelf, opening herself to his full length.

He didn't comment on it. The slow glides in and out gathered steam as their sounds rose. Bain's muscles tightened and loosened against her back, and his hands flexed and tightened against her waist.

Ari reveled in it. When Bain made love to her, he put everything into the act. And not just physically; he was single-minded, seemingly unconcerned with anything in the world but being inside her.

As if I have much of anything on my mind but having him inside me. That was the truth.

Bain's moans warmed her ear, and he leaned toward her and nipped at the lobe. "Come for me, baby. I want to go to work with my cock aching for more and obsessing over how good it was."

He said the most delicious things, words that made her wet, made her blood heat and her heart pound, and things that pushed her closer to climax. This was one of those times. Her body reached for the pinnacle that was so close.

"That's right. I feel that soft little pussy gearing up to purr for me."

Purring wasn't the word for it. Her pussy was a Mustang roaring to life around him. One more comment and she'd be full bore. And he knew that. Once Bain had learned how hot a few erotic promises and pillow talk made her, he'd been relentless.

"I started something this morning I didn't get to finish. Tonight, I'm going to have my tongue between those thighs in the shower."

The first precursors of climax forced a moan from her.

"Oh, you like that idea."

"Yes." She did. "I like sucking you while you're busy licking." There was nothing quite like an avid sixty-nine with Bain.

"After."

That one word shot her over, and Bain followed. Her muddled mind conceded that sex with him definitely beat sixty-nine.

That was the last coherent thought she managed. Everything after that was an explosion of color and sensation.

Bain's hands covered hers, and he pressed the length of his body to hers. Ari tried to force her breathing to ease, but that was difficult with her head spinning as it was.

"Maybe I should call off today and drive you."

The suggestion came out of the blue, shocking sense back into her rattled nerves. "You can't do that."

"Why not? Other guys do."

Because it makes me feel childish and pathetic. She'd always stood on her own feet. With David, it was a necessity, but now it was habit.

Bain won't want to hear that comparison. He didn't seem to like most of the comparisons she made, and it only reinforced how faulty her decision making had been all these years.

"Ari?"

"Didn't you say you had a meeting with Elias later this morning?" That was something you didn't just skip out on, and it was an obligation he couldn't ignore.

"Updates on R&D for the new chips," he grumbled. "What time is your appointment?"

"Eight-thirty." Ari knew his meeting was at nine. It went without saying that he couldn't be two places at one time. "I'll be fine. I don't need a ride. I'll take the base bus over."

"Take the cell with you...charged." There was an edge of an order in that. "If I can wiggle out early, I'll call you and meet you there."

She smiled. "Will do, Chief."

He swatted her backside lightly, then stopped to rub at the spot. "You don't call a man that loves you by his rank." It still amazed her how simply he'd fallen into saying it.

"Love you, too. Now get moving or you'll be marked U.A."

Bain left her body, but he didn't start washing. Instead, he turned her toward him and pressed a kiss to her forehead. "Take care of yourself, Ari. For me and for the kids."

She took a moment to snuggle into his body, then she planted a kiss on his lips and stepped out of the shower stall. "Will do. It's not easy for me...but I'm learning."

His smile said there was another reward coming later for that.

* * * *

"Still nothing that's jogged her memory?" Elias asked.

Bain sighed. "I don't get it. David played games, but he wouldn't have played one that left us without the pieces we need. This was too important to screw up, and when it came to the job, he was all business."

"It's going to take months...maybe years to recreate those chips, to even create something comparable to what is supposed to be in place."

"I know." And it bugged him. There had to be something missing. There had to be a clue he'd missed.

"You don't think there's any chance she's lying, do you?"

Bain tensed, his heart skittering at the idea of them labeling Ari a security risk or worse...a traitor. "Not a chance. Ari hates the Federalists. She'd never willingly help them."

Elias's next comment was preempted by a knock on the door.

"Enter," the Captain barked.

Commander Easten slid into the room and shut the door behind him. His gaze locked onto Bain momentarily then flitted away to Elias.

Bain stared at him, his personal alarm system screaming that something was wrong, something that could get dangerous fast enough to make his head spin.

"What do you need, Bill?" Elias asked.

Again, Easten's eyes flicked back and forth. "A call came in that I thought you ought to hear about." He clutched a slip of paper so hard, he was white-knuckling it.

Elias noticed that as well. His hand went out in silent order, and Easten set the paper in it, taking a single step back. The commander seemed to be studiously ignoring Bain; that kicked up his heart rate another dozen beats per minute.

"This has been confirmed?" Elias asked, adding another notch to the rising tension in the room.

Easten cleared his throat, as if he found speaking through the oppressive cloud as difficult as Bain found breathing through it.

"Yes. They're certain."

A moment of brittle silence followed.

"I've got it, Bill."

Easten nodded, shot one last pointed glance—*one of suspicion?*—at Bain, and left the office.

Bain resisted the urge to wipe his sweating palms on his khaki pants. "Captain?" he intoned. *Might as well be direct.* There was no question this had something to do with him...or Ari.

"Tell me, Carter. How close to this *situation* are you?"

"What situation? You know my team was coordinating with David's on design and implementation, before–"

"Personally," he qualified.

Bain considered that. "Back in the early days, David and I were friends," he admitted. "We all were. Gibbons, Riley, David, and me." He'd never made a secret of that.

"You're still friends with the others...Gibbons, Riley..."

He nodded, wondering at what that had to do with it.

"But not with David. Back in the early days, you were friends." He hesitated. "But not now."

Bain tried to follow his logic, without success. He had a witness to what happened to David. Surely, Elias wasn't accusing him of–

"Your falling out was over *her*, wasn't it? Aurora Evans?"

He paused...then nodded, still trying to understand what it had to do with the current situation.

"Did you fuck her? Is that why you're not friends anymore?"

Elias's blunt accusation fired his anger, and Bain did a slow five-count before answering. "Of course not. I wanted her, but she was with David. She wanted to stay with–"

"But now she's not with David," Elias stated, no less blunt or accusatory than his last statement.

Bain gaped at him, at a loss to fathom where the captain was going with it.

"Are you too close to the objective, Carter?"

"No. I know Ari. There's no–"

"So I gathered," he quipped.

Bain shook his head. "Why do I get the feeling we're having two different conversations here?" Something definitely didn't add up. Even if Elias suspected Bain was sleeping with Ari, he couldn't seriously believe Bain was terminally stupid...or a traitor.

"You went into that house on a mission," Elias snapped.

"And I'm doing my job," Bain countered. "Whatever David said, Ari has no clue what he meant by it."

"Doing your job." Elias sneered at that.

"Yes. I am–"

"I'm sure you've done a full cavity search, by now." There was yet another accusation couched in that.

Bain's head spun. "Are we talking about microchips or sex here?"

Elias closed his eyes, as if seeking patience. "You're admitting it then?"

"Admitting what? Only a fool agrees to something without knowing what he's accused of." If he was being accused of covering for some misdeed of David's or Ari's, Bain wasn't going down that way. If Elias meant their relationship, there was no crime in that.

Well...technically, they could try to throw the U.C.M.J. at him, but that was a long shot, at best. There were two consenting adults, after all, and neither one of them was married.

Elias's eyes opened, hot in some strong emotion. He waved the slip of paper between them. "This says Aurora Evans is pregnant...newly pregnant. I'm taking a wild guess that I don't have to look far for the father." He paused. "Do I?"

A smile pulled up at Bain's lips. With Ari's reproductive problems, he hadn't even considered the possibility.

Who says it was her problem? It might have been David mucking up the works.

The cause of her problem conceiving with David was a moot point. For now, Ari was his concern...Ari and their baby together.

"Carter? I'm waiting," Elias hinted.

"No. You've definitely found the father."

A muttered string of curses flowed from Elias's mouth.

"That hasn't dimmed my attention to *other* details. If Ari has the chips, I'll find them eventually. I don't doubt that she has no clue what David did with them."

"You're sure about that? You're sure you're not seeing what she wants you to see?" he challenged.

"Ari *wants* to find the chips. We've literally torn everything she carried with her apart, even the compass, pens... She's handed over her hiking boots.

Nothing. We did a full check on her van and its contents, before we even found her. Nothing.

"Maybe she lost it. Maybe she never had it. I don't know, but she's not lying."

"You're sure about her?" he repeated.

More sure than I am of you. But that wouldn't go over well. "Yes. I am."

Elias dropped the sheet of paper to the desk-top. "And what are you going to do about this?"

Bain indulged in a wide smile. "What I've wanted to do for the last fifteen years, if she'll have me."

"It's safe to say she's already had you." He raised a teasing brow.

"The first of many jokes, I'd bet." Bain glanced at the sheet of paper. "Uh...do you..."

"Dismissed. Get going."

Bain pushed to his feet.

"But, Carter..." Elias hesitated, seemingly discomfited.

He didn't look around. "Yes, Captain?"

"Be right about her. Be sure."

Bain didn't need to consider it. "Oh, I am."

* * * *

"I'm...uh...what?" Ari gripped the edge of the chair beneath her, her head in a flat spin.

"Pregnant," the doctor repeated.

"No. That's not–" Well, of course, it was *possible*, but it sure as hell wasn't probable. In sixteen years without birth control, there'd been only Lea. "An ear infection...or sinus. I always get dizzy with–"

197

"You are congested, Ms. Evans. You are also pregnant." He waited for some sign of understanding or acceptance from her.

Ari nodded, forcing herself to pay attention to what the doctor was saying.

"Considering your recent illness and the physical stresses of the preceding months, obstetrics will want to see you soon. I'll start you on prenatal vitamins right away." He looked up sharply, his eyes narrowing. "Unless you don't wish to have the baby," he hinted.

"Of course, I want to have the baby." Her voice sounded strange in her own ears.

Ari wouldn't dream of terminating, but what about Bain? They hadn't talked about the lack of condoms, past both of their assurances that there wasn't a risk of STDs involved. He'd probably assumed, as she had, that they were safe from a child.

The fertility treatments to conceive Lea, coupled with the lack of success without them for all the years after... *Hell, I haven't even had a period for four months.* It was hard to miss something you stopped having on the run...or when you were stressed or sick or...

"Ms. Evans?"

She snapped her gaze back to the doctor. "Yes?"

"I asked if you were sure."

"Yes. I'm sure."

Bain was another subject. Even David hadn't been overjoyed at the day-to-day realities of having a child, and he'd thrown himself into creating one.

In retrospect, she realized it was just one more thing to check off on David's list. Join the military—check. Get married—check. Have a kid—check. Work in the private sector—check. Just make sure none of it interferes with Saturday off—check.

"Okay, then. Let's get some more blood tests."

* * * *

Ari stepped into the house, peeled off her coat, hung it on the hooks by the door, then crossed to the couch and dropped onto it. She had two hours to decide how to broach this subject.

A sound from upstairs called her a liar. She checked the wall clock again. It wasn't even two, too early for Bain or any of the kids to be home. Her hope that she was hearing things was extinguished at the next sound. It was inside, though she couldn't decide which of the closer rooms it was in. Maybe Bain's...

Panic settled in, and she considered what her best move would be.

She patted the dead cell phone in her pocket, cursing herself for not checking the charge before she left. *Bain reminded me to, and I didn't.* It was a failing of hers, and they both knew it.

Call shore patrol...the M.P.s, base police...whoever was security on the mixed base? No. Since she didn't know the direct number, she'd have to call the base operator and wait to be transferred to them. That could take too long, and whoever was upstairs might overhear her.

She couldn't call the 9-1-1 operator, either. They'd have to send base police or make their way past the gate guards.

If Ari left, where would she go? To the neighbors, assuming any of them were home at this hour, and ask them to call? Probably a good idea. She rose and turned toward the door, half-lost in plans of doing just that.

Ari almost dismissed the next sound, but the change brought her back to the here and now. That sound wasn't upstairs. It was on the stairs...low on the stairs. Her heart pounding, she turned back...

And into Bain's arms. His lips covered hers, parting them, speeding her pounding heart for a new reason. The kiss was hot and hard, the type of kiss that promises you won't be wearing clothing for more than a few minutes. Just when Ari thought she'd end up pressed into the carpet, Bain peeling her jeans down, he broke away, smiling widely.

His voice was low and full of promise. "I've been waiting for you to get here."

How long will that last? Ari forced a deep breath, mentally preparing herself for his reaction, no matter what it might be.

He took her hands, leading her toward the stairs.

"Bain... There's something–"

"There's something I have to show you," he cut her off.

Ari climbed the stairs, always two steps behind him. Part of her wanted to put this off, to just enjoy what he had planned before she disrupted everything. Another part argued that there was no way she could relax into anything, until she told him.

They were nearly to the top of the stairs, when she forced herself to speak again. "Bain, I really should–"

"Just a minute," he promised.

She took a calming breath, prepared to insist that this was important.

Bain turned her left at the top of the stairs, whisking her toward their room. The nagging voice urged her to forget her news for a few minutes. She'd still be pregnant this evening...or tomorrow.

Coward. Tell him. "Bain..." Her voice failed her, as he passed by the bedroom. Ari glanced at the door, confused.

He stopped in front of the door to the small room Matt had been using before Mike came home to care for him, the one they'd discussed turning into a home office. "Me first?" he inquired.

Ari nodded, at a loss for how to begin anyway. She'd thought she had two hours to figure out something, after all.

Bain turned the knob and swung the door in.

For a long moment, she stayed trapped in his gaze, trying to analyze what she was seeing. She'd thought he was in a nearly manic up-mood, happy, bouncing on the balls of his feet. But it was more than that. There was something guarded about him. He was nervous, jittery.

As if in confirmation, his eyes slanted toward the now-open room, and she followed his line of sight, gasping in surprise.

The crib was set where Matt's bed had once been. It was a beautiful piece, light oak in a sleigh bed style. Something niggled at the back of her mind, a vague memory.

Ari ambled toward it, running a hand along the footboard. "I've seen this before," she mused. But...where?

"Good. It's the right one," he half-laughed, in what sounded like relief. "I'd hate to have to take it back."

She turned to him, trying to follow the conversation. "What?"

"You wanted this crib for Lea. I still remember the way you stared at it...the way you fussed with the quilt, before you moved on to the one you bought."

"Babies R Us," she managed. She'd forgotten that Bain had gone with her to bring the baby furniture home. It seemed strange that she'd forgotten that. Bain had always been around to help her with the little details in life, before she refused him.

He nodded. "You have no idea how close I came to buying it for you, just to watch your eyes light up."

Ari looked to the crib and then back to him, her mind working slowly to the answer. "You already know." She didn't question it. Why else would he buy a crib?

Bain nodded, waiting for her reaction, nearly squirming in place.

"How? I don't... Why did you..." A logical progression of thoughts was suddenly a pipe dream.

He crossed the room to her, enveloping Ari in one strong arm, guiding her head up with the opposite hand to capture her lips in a slow, solemn kiss. In the moment after he pulled his head back, his answer fanned over her lips. "Why? I'd hoped you'd know why, by now."

Her heart skipped in excitement, and forming an answer seemed tedious. "You're not upset?"

"Are you?"

Ari didn't know how to answer that. In the end, she managed a shaky answer of "unsure." Realizing how bad that sounded, she shook her head. "We didn't plan this. I didn't know what you'd..."

He took his time answering. "What I'd say or do?"

She didn't want to hurt him or insult him by comparing him to David, but he deserved an honest answer. "Yeah."

"Are you unsure about the baby?" He was serious, assessing.

"No." That was an easier question to answer.

A smile curved his lips up. "Then there's just one thing left we have to discuss."

"How you knew before I could tell you?"

The smile dimmed. "Let's just say that WesCom is still very interested in you...too interested, in my opinion."

A sliver of fear settled in her heart. What would Elias and the others do if they never found the chips? If they were still watching her, they didn't believe her.

* * * *

"I don't know where they are," Ari complained.

Her expression shifted from hurt to panic so fast, it made Bain's head spin.

"I know. I don't doubt that."

"They do. You won't be the one trying to throw me in jail."

Bain wrapped her in his arms, at a loss to reassure her. Elias and Easten didn't trust her. There was no denying that. He'd won a momentary reprieve from Elias. It would take time to convince the captain that Ari wasn't playing a game.

"What am I going to do, Bain?"

"Marry me."

Her breathing hitched. "What?"

"Marry me."

"What good will that do?"

"For Elias? No idea. Maybe something. Maybe nothing."

Ari looked up, seemingly at a loss.

"It's relatively simple. I don't give a shit what Elias thinks. This isn't about Elias. I didn't just buy a crib today. I've wanted to marry you for the last fifteen years. So...I'm asking."

She didn't seem to know how to reply to that.

"The only reason I didn't ask you earlier was that you were still getting used to the idea of being a widow. Maybe you still are. If you need time to decide, you do. No hard feelings if you don't just jump at the offer."

Ari nodded, seemingly deep in thought.

"Do you want held or space?" He'd asked that several times in the last few months. It probably wouldn't be the last time he had to.

She hesitated, then sank into his arms. "Held."

Bain smiled. It was the first time she'd said that outright. "Let's go to bed."

Ari stiffened in his arms.

"Just holding each other," he promised. "It's been a rough day."

"Sounds good."

"I'll even make dinner."

"That's a first," she teased.

"I have learned a few things in all these years."

* * * *

Ari stretched, opening her eyes to the sight of the empty bed. Faintly, she could hear the sound of voices from downstairs. A glance at the clock offered the explanation. She'd fallen asleep, and Bain had gotten up to meet the kids after school.

Her eyes locked on the ring box he'd left on the nightstand.

She lay there, working her way through their situation. At some indeterminate point in time, Ari had started thinking of the girls as "their" kids. She'd invested more in the idea of Bain as a father to Lea than she'd ever invested in David as one, and it seemed Bain had gladly stepped into the role...as consistently and competently as military life would allow, and his current duty station was certainly more stable than submarines had ever been.

We've become a family. So why does the thought of marrying Bain scare the crap out of me?

Is it because my marriage to David was such a failure? That was an unpalatable thought. Bain wasn't David. She wasn't punishing Bain for David's shortcomings, was she?

She'd like to say she was simply enjoying the freedom of not being someone's wife, but that wasn't accurate. She was more a wife to Bain now than she'd been to David for years.

When he'd stopped showing up to dinner regularly, Ari had stopped catering to what David liked to eat and had started preparing what she and Lea liked. *When was the last time I concerned myself with changing a recipe to make it palatable to David?* Too long ago to remember.

But she'd cooked to Bain's tastes without a thought of it being an imposition to do it. And he appreciated it, where David had simply expected it. In fact, Bain had only missed dinner unexpectedly twice in as many months, and he'd not only called to let her know but also apologized for it, though it wasn't his fault he'd been held up at work.

So why am I so shaken by the idea of marrying him? Logically, it didn't make sense.

As if love is logical.

That had been half the problem with David. Too much in their marriage had been logical, convenient, discussed or at least demanded and expected, reasoned...scheduled. With Bain, it was a wild ride.

Stop being logical. Love wasn't logical, so why was she so busy trying to make it logical?

Ari picked up the ring box and turned it in her hand. She and Bain were already living like they were married. What would the ring change? Not much that she could fathom.

At the very least, their baby wouldn't be considered a bastard.

That's logical. It wasn't completely logical. It was an emotional issue, so she let it stand.

What about the military's suspicions? That was logical, but it was also important. Technically speaking, she couldn't conceive of marrying her putting him any more at risk than he already was, but it would protect their kids.

And it would make sure the military provided medical for them all when she was no longer of use for finding their precious microchips.

Logical! she berated herself.

Okay. Let's consider something completely illogical. Do I want to marry Bain? What does the idea make me feel?

Ari didn't have to consider that for long. She wanted nothing more than to wear the ring he'd offered.

That decided, she put it on and headed down the stairs.

* * * *

Bain looked up at Ari's descent into the living room, offering a smile for her from over Josie's math homework.

She looked much better than she had when they'd retired to the bed. Ari was rested now, less stressed. The final change took a moment to sink in.

She's wearing the ring. "Does this mean what I think it does?" he chanced asking. He hoped it did.

"Yes."

That one word made his day. Bain pushed to his feet and wound a path between the girls to reach her, ignoring their confusion for the moment.

He leaned down to kiss her, and Ari wrapped her arms around his neck to press to him. Restraining himself to a slow exploration when he wanted something hot and blatant was difficult, but he managed it.

Josie let out an "eww" that reinforced her age.

Lea snorted. Before Bain could question the move, she answered him.

"Took you long enough, Bain. I was starting to think you were leading my mom on."

Ari started laughing, and she broke off the kiss. Her dark eyes glittered in amusement. "I'm not complaining."

Lea's voice was full of her father's sarcasm. "Good. Then I don't have to keep my promise to find a weapon and make him pay."

Chapter Eleven

November 30th

"Mommy, mommy, mommy!" Josie shouted the mantra, running into the room and ducking behind Ari.

It was a move she'd seen before. "What did you—"

"Mom!" The kitchen door banged open behind her daughter's hand.

Lea's voice set Ari's teeth on edge. *This is why people say to stop at one. And I'm bringing another into the fray?* "What did Josie–"

"It was an accident," Josie wailed.

"You were in my room." Lea reached for her.

Josie ducked to Ari's other side. "I didn't mean it."

"You little–"

"Enough," Ari ordered.

Both girls fell silent. Lea held her left hand fisted at her side, her muscles strung tight in fury. Ari considered that; it was an unusual reaction for Lea. Josie pulled at the back of Ari's T-shirt, spurring her to speech.

"Now... Josie, you went in Lea's room?"

"Yes." The answer rumbled against Ari's back.

"Are you supposed to?" she pressed.

Lea shot her a look of frustration, and Ari warned her off with a sharp look in return.

"No."

"E.M.I....and we'll discuss this later. At the very least, you owe Lea an apology. You may owe her more than that. Now, get going."

"Mom," Lea complained.

"It's not settled yet," Ari assured her.

"It better not be," she grumbled.

Josie circled Ari and Lea, shooting a nervous glance at the younger, then fled for the stairs. Her footsteps pounded away and up; in the distance, a door slammed.

Lea took a deep breath, and Ari echoed it.

"It wasn't just going in your room." Ari didn't question it.

"No." Her daughter didn't offer any more information.

"Do you want to tell me about it?"

Lea raised her fisted hand, staring at it in undisguised misery.

"Lea?"

"She broke it."

That still didn't explain it. Lea was notoriously unconcerned about her personal belongings, probably because she'd left everything behind once.

"Broke what, Lea?"

Her hand opened, palm up, revealing the bracelet inside.

Ari nodded, her heart aching. Lea *hadn't* left everything behind. The bracelet was the single possession her daughter had from before the call.

"She broke it, Mom." Tears welled in her eyes.

"We'll get it fixed. Jewelry can be repaired." No matter what it took, Ari would get it fixed.

"And...if they can't fix it?" There was a note of desperation in her tone.

"I'll get you a new one...one just like the old one." *I'll have it reproduced, if I have to.*

Lea's hand closed on the bracelet. "You can't replace it," she choked. "It will never be the same. Don't you see?"

"Because it came from home?" Lea had adjusted so well here. She'd even accepted Bain into their lives. Had Ari been wrong all this time? "Lea...we can make a new h—"

"Because it was a gift."

"What?" What was Lea talking about?

"It was a gift from Dad. It's not like he can give me another gift, Mom. Not ever. It's the only one I have left."

Ari's head spun. "We'll fix it. I promise you, we'll fix it."

A tear slid down Lea's cheek. "I shouldn't have taken it off. I promised."

"P-pr..." Ari cleared her throat, her heart thundering in rising suspicion. "Who did you..." *Scratch that. She promised David.* "*What* did you promise your father?"

"I promised never to let it out of my sight."

"Never let it out of your sight," Ari whispered.

Lea nodded.

Ari put out her hand. "I'll fix it, Lea. Bain and I will. You have my word on that. We'll fix it."

The bracelet settled in her palm, and Lea walked away with a last look of longing back at the gift from David. Ari stared at it, torn between relief and hurt.

It was all about Lea. For years, Ari had suspected David only stayed for two reasons: his commitment to never losing and his daughter. Though she'd like to believe he'd only given the bracelet to Lea, because he believed Ari would throw it back at him in anger, she knew it wasn't true. In the end, David thought only of Lea.

* * * *

Bain strolled through the kitchen doorway, his smile fading at the sight of Ari.

She sat at the table, staring out the window, her hands clasped in her lap. There was no dinner cooking. There were no children romping and listening to music or watching television. The silence of the house registered with him, sending a shiver up his spine. Something was very wrong.

He settled in the chair next to her. "Ari?"

She shifted toward him but didn't look at him. "Tell me again?"

"Tell you..." Something major had gone down, but Bain couldn't fathom what it was.

"About David."

An edge of something hard and unforgiving sent a slice of cold through his gut. Bain nodded, forcing his jaw to unclench. "He contacted us, but he ran into a Federalist scout first."

Her head turned, and his heart stuttered at her look of apathy.

"No. Tell me what David said."

"He was his typical sparkling self," Bain joked weakly. *He was being a bastard. He knew I wanted Ari, that I'd always want Ari.*

And damned if Bain wasn't the better man; from what he could see, she and Lea had been neglected far too long. Weekend Daddy-dates weren't enough for any kid, and Ari had had less of him than that.

"About the chips," she qualified.

Surprise stole his voice for a moment. Bain cleared his throat. "He said he gave them to you...hid them in something and told you never to let it out of your hands." The memory niggled at him. "No...sight. Never let it out of your sight."

Something told him he had to be specific, and her flinch seemed to support that theory. Ari closed her eyes, looking weary. Before he could question the response, she continued.

"He said my name?" That seemed to surprise her.

"I gave them to her."

Hadn't that bothered me, at the time? The fact that David never said Ari's name? Bain had written it off as their estrangement, once he'd known about it. He'd written it off as David's animosity at the idea of Bain with Ari, before then.

"Bain?" Tears threatened in that prod for an answer.

He shook his head in a negative reply. "He said 'her.' I assumed he meant you." His head spun. "Was there another woman?" Did she believe that?

For that matter, what would make her consider it now? If she'd thought it, why hadn't she said it earlier?

If it was true, why hadn't David made that clear to Bain? He couldn't have lied to get Bain to go after Lea and Ari, at the expense of the plan. David hadn't been that crazy. Had he?

A bark of laughter escaped her lips, followed by a half-swallowed sob. "He never said my name. I thought so."

Bain ached for her. So there *was* another woman. "Ari..." But what could he say to her to ease that pain?

Her fisted hand rose between them, curled fingers up. He stared at it, his mind making tired circles.

"It has to come back perfect. I need your promise that it will. If it can't be fixed, we have to recreate it so perfectly she never knows it's not the original."

Bain met her eyes, noting her determination in unease. "What has to?"

Realization hit him like four hundred volts, and he panned his gaze to her fist. "You have them." *The chips. She had them all along. No...someone else had them, and now Ari is in possession of them.*

"Promise me."

Whoever it was, Ari was determined not to disappoint her. "I promise. Completely restored." If she had the chips, they were worth her weight in gold. Whatever had to be preserved could be fabricated again, if necessary.

Ari's hand opened, revealing a silver and amber bracelet. For a moment, Bain wracked his brains for where he'd seen it before.

"Lea," he breathed. It was nothing special, likely a fifteen or twenty-dollar piece of costume jewelry, but she always wore it. "She never lets it out of her sight." Lea only removed it for swim practice and meets.

Ari offered it to him. "It was never about me."

He considered that. "No. It was."

She stared at him, seemingly lost.

"It's a package deal, Bainbridge."

"That's one thing he was clear about. Between David and me, it has always been about you."

Ari's hand closed, and she nestled into his chest. Bain wrapped his arms around her, uncertain what to say to ease her pain.

Her voice teased at his throat. "Then the best man won...and so did I."

About the Author

Brenna Lyons wears many hats, sometimes all on the same day: former president of EPIC, author of more than 100 published works, owner of Fireborn Publishing, columnist, special needs teacher, wife, mother...and member in good standing of more than 60 writing advocacy groups.

In her first ten years published in novel-length, she's won 3 EPIC e-Book Awards (out of 15 finalists) and finaled for 3 PEARLS (including one Honorable Mention, second to NY Times Bestseller Angela Knight), 2 CAPAS, and a Dream Realm Award. She's also taken Spinetingler's Book of the Year for 2007.

Brenna writes in 26 established worlds plus stand-alones, poetry, articles and essays. She's a bestseller in indie/e fantasy and horror, straight genre and cross-genres thereof. Brenna has been termed "one of the most deviant erotic minds in the publishing world...not for the weak." (Rachelle for Fallen Angels Reviews) Milieu-heavy dark work is practically Brenna's calling card, with or without the erotic content.

She teaches classes in everything from POV studies to advanced editing, networking to marketing. Brenna enjoys hearing from people who read her work and can be reached by e-mail.

Website: http://www.brennalyons.com/

Facebook: http://www.facebook.com/brenna.lyons

Email: brennalyons4168@live.com

Also by this Author

STAR MAGES
The Master's Lover

XXAN WAR
Daahan Rising
Crossbred Son
Raashh Decisions

Enslaved
All I Want for Christmas is You
Fates Magic
All's Fair...
Black Sail
Mama's Tales
Dream Walk
Unexpected Daddy
Phaze in Verse
We Shall Live Again
May the Best Man Win
Nevermore
Marked
And It Was Good

Available from **Mundania Press**

STAR MAGES
Written in the Stars

Fairy Dreams
Monsters of Myth Anthology

Available from **Under the Moon**

RENEGADES SERIES
TYGERS
Renegade's Run
Max Sec

URBAN GRIMM
Catch Me, If You Can
Three Wishes
Temptation of Eve

With Great Power
Undead in Blue
Evil Overlords Union Issue #1 Anthology
Undead Embrace
"Playing Games" in *Forbidden Love: Bad Boys*
"Marked" in *Forbidden Love: Wicked Women*
"The Master's Lover" in *Forbidden Love: Sacred Bands*

Available from ***Logical Lust***

"Mine for the Night" in *The Cougar Book* Anthology

Available from ***Coming Together Charity Anthologies***

INSTINCT SERIES
"Foundling" in *Coming Together: Into the Light* Anthology

"Claim Mate" (available separately and as part of the *Coming Together: Against the Odds* Anthology)
"The Fire God's Woman" in *Coming Together: Under Fire* Anthology

Available ***self-published***

KEGIN SERIES
Earth-Born Lord
Graham: Training the Earth-Born Lord

NIGHT WARRIORS
Claiming a Lady
Stone Lord

Mother's Son

COLOR OF LOVE
A Safe Heart

Snapshots from a Poet's Life

Award-Winning Books

EPPIE/EPIC eBOOK AWARDS WINNERS
Coming Together: Against the Odds- 2010
Time Currents- 2010
Coming Together: Into the Light- 2011

EPPIE/EPIC eBOOK AWARDS FINALISTS
Fion's Daughter- 2004
Collected Poems: Book One- 2005 (now titled *Snapshots of a Poet's Life*)
Renegade's Run- 2005
Rites of Mating- 2006
All I Want for Christmas- 2006
Phaze in Verse- 2008
"The Fire God's Woman" in *Coming Together: Under Fire*- 2009
Three Wishes- 2010
Matchmaker's Misery- 2010
The Cougar Book- 2011
The Master's Lover- 2011
Bride Ball- 2011

DREAM REALM AWARDS FINALIST
Last Chance for Love- 2003

PEARL HONORABLE MENTION
Night Warriors- 2004

PEARL FINALISTS
Schente Night- 2003 (now included in *The Last of Fion's Daughters*)
König Cursebreakers- 2004 (now titled *Will of the Stone*)

JOYFULLY REVIEWED BEST BOOKS OF 2010
Written in the Stars- 2010

SPINETINGLER'S BOOK OF THE YEAR 2007

NOBODY: An Anthology of Dark Fiction- 2007 (Brenna's pieces of the anthology can be found in *Beyond the Veil*)

TRS's CAPA FINALISTS
Ultimate Warriors- 2004 (Brenna's portion is now available as *With Great Power*)
Written in the Stars

LOVE ROMANCE AND MORE CAFÉ BOOK OF THE YEAR RUNNER UP
Last Chance for Love- 2008

ROAD TO ROMANCE REVIEWERS' CHOICE AWARD
Prophecy: Revelations- 2004

LOVE ROMANCES REVIEWERS' CHOICE AWARD
Black Sail- 2003

ROMANCE JUNKIES BOOK CLUB STAFF PICK
TYGERS- 2003

FALLEN ANGELS ROMANCE RECOMMENDED READ
Devon's Price-2005 (now available in *Bearing Armen*)

JOYFULLY RECOMMENDED READ
Fairy Dreams- 2008
The Last of Fion's Daughters- 2009

TREBLE HEART FINALIST
Prophecy: Revelations- 2003